An *Atom* Book

First published in Great Britain by Atom 2003

Based on concepts devised by Ben Sharpe
Story by A. J. Butcher

A CIP catalogue record for this book
is available from the British Library.

ISBN 1 904233 14 7

Typeset in Cochin by M Rules
Printed and bound in Great Britain by Bookmarque Ltd, Croydon

Atom
An imprint of
Time Warner Books UK
Brettenham House
Lancaster Place
London WC2E 7EN

Sixty years from now, north of Boston USA, there's a school that's more than it seems.

People whisper the name of the Deveraux College like a secret, and wonder at what they've heard. They know the school was founded by Jonathan Deveraux, one of the wealthiest men in the world, and that he is rumoured to live on the premises but hasn't been seen in the flesh for fifteen years. They know that the school is so exclusive, so select, that not even the sons of Presidents or the daughters of rock stars can get in. They know that the College's literature talks of the 'exceptionally talented', but exceptionally talented at what? Nothing more is revealed. Ultimately, all people really know is where the college is and what it looks like. But only from the outside.

You approach it through grounds the size of Rhode Island, mostly forest. If you're alert, you might notice the branches of the trees stirring, moving, even on breezeless days — keeping an arboreal eye on your progress. Because instead of bark or sap, the branches of the trees at Deveraux contain circuitry and sensors, carefully monitoring the presence of each and every trespasser on College land.

At last the forest falls away and you see the school itself ahead of you. It's as if the centuries have fallen away, too. The Deveraux College is a sprawling, gothic fortress perfect for hidden rooms, and dungeons, and screams in secret corridors. The kind of place where you wouldn't want the power to fail in the middle of the night and where you'd be quite keen to wear a cross around your neck, and maybe a few cloves of garlic for good measure.

Of course, you could pause there, if you didn't feel like going any further, and watch Deveraux's students at sport on the playing fields. There's always a football game going on. Always. And if you stand watching it long enough, you'll realise that it's the same plays repeated, time after time, like an endless rehearsal. And that realisation might trouble you, unless you already know that all you're observing are holograms, designed to project an illusion of normality.

The true business of the Deveraux College goes on inside.

Through the great oak doors that open automatically. Past the receptionist who, despite her pensionable age, could kill you in a dozen different ways with her bare and wrinkled hands. Past the phantom students forever on their way to lessons that never start. Into one of the many book-lined studies which, if you press the spine of the book that is not a book, proves not in actual fact to be a study, either, but an elevator. An elevator that takes you down, beneath the ground, behind the facade, to the place where the Deveraux College in many ways ceases to be, to a school which has been christened by its students with a different name.

Spy High.

There are uniforms here, but no blazers or ties or regulation-length skirts. At Spy High, students don gleaming silver ShockSuits, and if you want to know why they're called that, try jumping someone wearing one in a dark alley: you're likely to find it an electrifying experience. There are classes here, too, but little that would feature at other educational institutions, unless spycraft, history of espionage, advanced computer hacking, enemy disabling techniques and the handling of weapons of mass destruction suddenly become essentials of the curriculum. There is a holo-gym for all kinds of physical combat training, a virtual reality chamber equipped with the latest cyber-cradles, and study and recreational facilities of every description.

And then there is the Hall of Heroes. A hushed location, this, a place for reverence and reflection. The plaque on the wall spells out its purpose in glittering golden letters: 'Dedicated to the graduates of the Deveraux College. To those who risk their lives for the sake of tomorrow.' At the far end of the Hall, the Fallen are commemorated, those who have perished in the ceaseless battle between the forces of good and the agents of evil. Their holographic forms hover in beams of light, their names emblazoned beneath, as though they are standing sentinel still against the darkness of the world. If nothing else, they are a reminder to the students of Spy High that they haven't been chosen to play games, but to be active participants in a deadly struggle that could cost them their very lives.

A group of students is entering the Hall of Heroes now. The tall blond boy leading the way is Ben Stanton, while the equally tall and equally blonde girl whose hand he's holding, that's Lori Angel. They're what you might call close, and not just because, other than the obvious physiological differences between them, they look virtually identical. The rest of their team follows on. The African-American girl, Cally Cross, with her dreadlocks impeccably in place as ever, she seems interested, her bright, intelligent eyes missing nothing. Jake Daly, who slouches alongside her, wears a rather more bored expression beneath his tangle of black hair, but you would be unwise to underestimate him. Look more closely and you'll see that his dark, even swarthy features and compact, muscular body exude power and intensity. He's someone you'd want on your side in a fight. You might not think the same could be said of Eddie Nelligan, red-haired, looking like he's just got out of bed, grinning at some secret joke, but he's not here by accident, either. Then there's the last of the group, keeping a slight distance from the others as if she doesn't quite belong: Jennifer Chen, green-eyed and lithe-limbed like a cat.

Ben directs his team-mates to the far end of the Hall to the Fallen, where the memorials are of a more auspicious kind.

'Here they are,' he breathes as if referring to the saints, 'the past winners of the Sherlock Shield.'

Mounted on plinths like exhibits in a museum, the trophies immortalised each passing year's most successful student team at Spy High – those awarded the Sherlock Shield. The team members' faces, beaming as if in pride at their achievements, rotate slowly and three-dimensionally alongside their engraved names.

Ben, though, seems more interested in the plinth at the end of the row, the one that so far lacks a trophy to be placed upon it. 'And here's ours,' he promises. 'Here's where Bond Team's shield will go.' His eyes sparkle as he imagines it, the honour, the glory, for the others as well as for himself, though as team leader, of course . . . 'That's our target for this term. That's our goal. To win the Sherlock Shield.' He turns to his team-mates. 'Anybody want to say different?'

Nobody does. Lori, as ever, is the dutiful girlfriend and squeezes his hand supportively. Jake Daly is less impressed, but from the terse nod of his head, no less committed. Cally says 'I'm with you' and Eddie says nothing, which the others assume means he's being serious for once. Jennifer's silence, too, is interpreted as agreement, allowing Ben to feel good about himself and inwardly applaud his idea of bringing Bond Team down to the Hall of Heroes.

But, in reality, Jennifer's silence denotes neither agreement nor disagreement, because she hasn't heard a word that's been said. The Sherlock Shield is of no interest to her whatsoever. Jennifer Chen has something else on her mind, something else entirely.

She knew she was dreaming. The smile on her face and the laugh in her throat kind of gave it away. She didn't do much of either these days. Besides, she was back home again, and Mum and Dad and little Shang were with her, and the light in the room was golden and without shadows. She was where she couldn't possibly be, with people who couldn't possibly be there, but Jennifer didn't care.

If only it could last forever.

She hugged her parents and her little brother, held them close, and it seemed as though she could feel them solidly against her own body, their hearts beating strongly in their chests. Which was impossible.

And the sound that she could hear was not the hearts of her family in any case, not even her own. It was the thumping of dull, hollow blows on the door. (Somehow, the door was in the room, though Jennifer seemed to remember it had used to be at the end of the hall). It was the flat, fatal beating on the door, like dirt heaped on a coffin. And her parents heard it too, and little Shang, and they knew what they had to do.

They turned to the door and the sudden darkness it held, gaping like a grave. They turned from Jennifer.

'No, don't go!' Her protests were useless. They went unheard. 'Mum! Dad! Don't leave me!' The sound of the pounding filled the air.

Her parents were at the door. She couldn't see their faces.

'Don't let him in! Don't let him in!'

But they did. And night entered the room like the serpent in paradise. And though Jennifer clutched for her family with desperate fingers, she was too late. In her dream as in life, she was always too late.

At least she didn't wake up screaming any more.

Familiarity had provided her with some degree of self-control. She didn't want to disturb the others as she had done several times during last term – she still sensed Lori looking at her strangely, suspiciously, from time to time. But she had to get up. Her bedside clock said three am. There was going to be no more sleep for her tonight.

Jennifer slipped out of bed and stole to the bathroom, locked the door softly behind her. Just in time. All of a sudden the sobs came, deep, racking groans of grief, and she fell to her knees by the toilet and she knew she was going to be violently ill.

The trouble was, when it was over, she didn't feel any better.

And she hadn't forgotten what was imminent, either.

A cautious knocking at the door. 'Jen? Are you all right in there?' Lori, practising her night nurse routine. 'I thought I heard . . .?'

'No. I'm fine.' She was surprised how fluent the lie was, how strong her voice seemed. 'Just a bit of an upset stomach, I think. I'll live.' Bitterly.

And the twisted part of her wanted to scream out: 'Leave me alone! Go away! What do you know? What do you care?'

And in the mirror in the bathroom, Jennifer's face splintered into tears.

Routine. Daniel Daniels hated it.

Routine was turning him psychic. Daniel Daniels reckoned that he could now predict precisely what he'd be doing at any given point in the working day next week, next month, next year, for the rest of his natural life. Routine was making a robot out of him as surely as if he'd had those cybernetic limbs fitted that were all the rage these days. It was making him a cog in a machine.

If only something unusual would happen, a little bit of the unexpected.

But it was likelier that a meteorite might fall on his head.

Take this morning, for example (and Daniel Daniels wished someone would). Six o'clock: the alarm and his bed's automatic sheet retraction service. Seven o'clock: leave the house wearing the suit that might as well be a prison uniform, though it cost significantly more. Seven-thirty: catch the hoverbus into the city, have to stand due to congestion problems reducing the number of services. Eight-thirty: arrive at the Wainwright Building where he'd worked for the past twenty years and was likely to have to work for the next twenty, no chance of parole.

Have his retina scanned for security purposes (though people were more likely to want to break out of the Wainwright Building rather than in). Be recognised by the doorman program and greeted with a cyber-smile: 'Good morning, Mr Daniels. How are you today?' Plan one day on telling the doorman program exactly how he was today.

Enter the elevator. Watch Baines call out from across the marble foyer: 'Hey, hold those doors!' Wait for him to slip inside: 'Hey, nearly didn't make it today.' Feel the desperate urge to punch him on the nose. Feel the very real need to scream as he says 'Gentlemen, which floors?' as if he hadn't been pressing those same buttons at the same time since the beginning of the world.

Walk with colleagues along the corridor of the seventieth, exchanging pleasantries and wishing they were dead. March with colleagues into separate offices, silent and civil glass doors sealing them in with preset efficiency.

Start the day. Pray for it to end.

'Morning, Marilyn.' At least Daniel Daniels didn't have to disguise the gloom in his voice for his computer. It responded to the vibration of his vocal chords, not his mood.

'Hello, Daniel,' cooed the computer, activating itself obediently. 'What would you like to do today? I'm always open to suggestions.' Laughter tinkled from the screen as the face of Daniel Daniels' favourite movie icon of the last century winked coyly at him. The Marilyn Monroe program was one of the few things that made his day bearable.

'You'd better read me my e-mails first, Marilyn,' he said, not that he expected anything exciting to be amongst them.

He was nearly right.

'And one final message,' Marilyn concluded several minutes later, 'but it's not addressed to you personally, Daniel. It's not addressed to anyone by name. Should I still read it?'

'What does it say, then?' He was scarcely even curious. But for a strange second, Daniel Daniels was distracted. What was that he'd just heard? From another office close by. Had he just heard what he thought he'd heard? A scream?

'It's simply addressed to the World of Order,' said Marilyn.

'Read it anyway.' It couldn't have been a scream, but Daniel Daniels could see others standing in their own offices, all looking in the same direction and with equal puzzlement. Towards Baines' room. And was that Baines in there, banging on unyielding glass to be let out? Why would he be doing that?

Behind him, Marilyn was giggling. 'Oh, this is an odd one,' she was saying. 'I don't really understand it.'

And now Harper, too, in the next office but one. That look on his face, it was like sheer terror . . .

Behind Daniel Daniels, Marilyn was giggling, though her voice seemed lower now, darker and grating. He turned in time to see her face blister and blacken, like it was being cremated. Her voice could no longer be heard. Something else was in the computer.

'Your time is over, little man,' the something scowled. 'The world you know, the world of order, is coming to an end. Prepare to greet a new age, the Age of CHAOS.'

'A virus,' Daniel Daniels gasped to himself as a dark and terrible shape took form on the computer screen. 'It's a virus.'

Then his machine exploded.

It seemed to start a chain reaction, explosions bursting from one office after another like an incendiary roll call. Daniel Daniels was thrown against the door by the detonation, but he was essentially unharmed. For a second, he even began to feel relief. Until the ceiling above him started to hiss and buckle and rupture, and cables spilled from it like black intestines. They snapped and swayed and sparked and Daniel Daniels knew that if any of them so much as touched him, down at the morgue they'd be identifying him by his dental records.

The mechanism to release the door didn't work, of course. It was computer controlled. The virus had infected it, too. Manual operation was impossible. He was trapped. Daniel Daniels' colleagues were finding the same problem. They were all of them screaming now, mad with panic, pounding on unbreakable glass as the murderous cables spilled into their cubicles, poised to strike, like snakes.

An electric flash, blinding, white. An unfeasibly high scream. A sizzling like cindered steak. And Daniel Daniels' bulging eyes registered that Harper was no longer trying to escape. He wasn't the only one, either. The cables were striking with deadly accuracy – as though they too were under virus control. He saw poor Baines throttled, gurgling his horror, yanked into the air jerking like a puppet. And Daniel Daniels knew it would be his own turn soon. *What could he do?*

His chair. The glass. It was a chance. He seized it and swung, clumsily but with all the strength a man in the last minutes of life could muster – aimed it at the door.

Which slid open. Like all he'd really had to do was ask politely. The chair's momentum sent both it and Daniel Daniels spinning out of the office and sprawling humiliatingly on the floor. Daniel Daniels couldn't speak for the chair, but he didn't mind in the slightest. There was nobody else alive to see him, anyway.

He scrambled to his feet, scurried for the elevator. There were the doors ahead of him.

He was sobbing to himself. If somehow he got out of this still breathing, if somehow he survived, he'd never criticise routine again. He'd be happy to lead an ordered, regimented, pre-programmed life for the rest of his days. Happy? He'd be ecstatic.

The elevator doors saw him coming and opened obligingly.

The unusual? The unexpected? Daniel Daniels hated them both.

He dived for the safety of the elevator, and maybe he'd been blinded by his tears of relief, or maybe he didn't look, or maybe he didn't even care. But Daniel Daniels dived seventy floors straight down.

The elevator wasn't there.

'**F**inal pair, take your positions,' snapped Corporal Randolph Keene. 'Ben Stanton and Simon Macey.' He spat out their names like pieces of gristle, as though he harboured a personal grudge against both of them.

Understandable enough in the case of Macey, Ben thought, but Keene ought to be demonstrating a little more respect towards himself. He'd soon be showing him why.

Ben and Simon approached the Wall, cheered on by their respective team-mates. Ben could even hear Jake Daly whooping encouragement, any differences between them put aside (if not quite forgotten) for the duration of the competition. Bond Team versus Solo Team. Ben Stanton versus Simon Macey. It was always going to come down to this.

'Break a leg, Simon,' Ben said.

'Break your neck, Stanton,' came the response.

Ben grinned. For secret agents, emotions were bad. Emotions were baggage. They weighed you down, muddled your thoughts, got in the way between you and what had to be done. A secret agent had to repress emotions, eliminate them. Macey wasn't doing that. He was hating Ben instead of focusing on the Wall. It meant he'd lose.

Ben sprayed the clingskin on the boots of his ShockSuit, and liberally onto his hands. The clear, gelatinous substance encased his skin like a tight and invisible glove. Ben closed his fists, rubbed his palms together. He couldn't feel any stickiness at all, yet the clingskin was strong enough and adhesive enough to allow him to scale the Wall with no further artificial aid. 'Look on it as a kind of human glue,' they'd been taught.

'What are you ladies waiting for? An invitation to dance?' Keene again. 'Take your positions before we all die of boredom.'

They stood at the foot of the Wall, though what they had to climb wasn't really just a *wall*, of course. Most walls tend to be built from the ground up, for safety reasons if nothing else. The Wall here, in Training Chamber Two at Spy High, had been constructed from the roof (a long, long way above them, its lights like stars) and extended down, and maybe the money had run out but it hadn't quite managed to reach the floor. The Wall hovered just above the boys' heads. It was sheer and it glistened darkly.

'On your marks,' barked Keene.

Ben tensed. Out of the corner of his eye he saw Lori urging him on. She'd done her bit for the cause, winning her race against Solo Team's Sonia Dark. So had Jake and Cally. Only Eddie, predictably, and Jennifer, surprisingly, had lost.

'Set.'

Like a spring, Ben told himself, crouching. Be like a spring.

So the score was three-two in Bond Team's favour. Just Ben and Macey to go. If Ben won, Bond Team won. If Ben won, Bond Team took a vital advantage in the race for the Sherlock Shield. There was nothing else for it. He *had* to win.

'Leap!'

Ben did, powering up with his legs. He slammed his hands against the smooth surface of the Wall, felt the clingskin holding him there without effort. He raised his feet to make contact with the Wall as well, even as the structure began to lean, began to move, a slow motion toppling, its angle to the floor gradually reducing from ninety degrees downwards, increasing the pressure of gravity on those attempting to climb it. On the Wall, even when aided by clingskin, technique was everything.

Ben trusted his technique. He'd paid attention in class. He'd practised hard. He thrust himself upwards, higher, sliding his hands and feet over the slickness of the Wall, never once breaking contact with it, spreading his fingers wide so that the clingskin could touch the maximum area possible. That was the trick. Press yourself as close to the Wall as to a girl you've always fancied and never let go, never give the clingskin a chance to stop doing its job. And focus, concentrate. Stick to your task, literally.

Ben slithered up the Wall.

It lowered to eighty-five degrees. Eighty. Macey was in hot pursuit. His leap had been as tall as Ben's but he'd scrabbled a little with his feet. He was already behind. Ben took further heart from this, reached up with his limbs perfectly synchronised. His heart raced. The roof was closer than the floor. *Seventy-five degrees. Seventy . . .*

Ben felt gravity plucking at him, for the first time felt a slight strain on the clingskin. If he wasn't careful, a hand or a foot could peel off the Wall like a sticking plaster from the flesh and then he'd fall. Ben Stanton had not joined Spy High to fall.

Sixty-five degrees. Sixty.

Was Macey gaining? How could that be? Macey was a loser, so obviously a loser that Ben half-expected it to be tattooed across his forehead. But he *was* gaining.

Fifty-five degrees.

He had to try something, confirm his advantage. Ben slanted sideways, cutting across what would have been Simon Macey's natural route up the Wall. It was like one car swerving in front of another, and just as the second car would likely have to brake unexpectedly hard to avoid an accident, so Simon Macey's upward rhythm was also interrupted.

'What . . .?' Macey drew his right hand from the Wall. It was enough. 'No!' Gravity grabbed him and pulled.

Ben looked down with triumph in his eyes. 'Not sticking around, Simon? Too bad.'

'Stanton!' Macey threatened. He lashed out with his hand, clutched for Ben's leg. Didn't make it. With a howl of defeat, Simon Macey dropped from the Wall and plunged to the floor. He'd be all right, of course. The floor was softly padded to avoid physical injury. The only part of Simon Macey that would be hurt would be his pride. Which was exactly how Ben liked it.

Fifty degrees. Forty-five. But angles didn't matter now. Ben slickly, smoothly, slid his way to the top of the Wall, hauled himself to the victor's platform, raised his arms aloft. Below him, the little people cheered. He just hoped the cameras had been on.

Lori ran to Ben first, hugged him, kissed him. The others didn't run, though they did walk kind of quickly, and they stopped short of a hug and a kiss too, which in the case of Jake and Eddie particularly, was only to be welcomed. There was a unanimous chorus of well dones and other variations on the theme.

'You sure showed us failures how to do it,' acknowledged Eddie, whose own effort at the Wall had been of the dangling helplessly variety.

'Well,' said Ben, 'somebody had to.'

'Modesty as well,' observed Jake ironically, nudging Jennifer. 'What would we do without him?'

Jennifer replied with a vapid half-smile, making Jake frown. All right, so she'd fallen from the Wall too, but it just didn't seem that that was troubling her. There was something else. Jake sensed it.

The students suddenly realised that Senior Tutor Elmore Grant had arrived.

'Were you watching us, sir?' Ben asked, clearly expecting an affirmative reply supported by praise. 'Did you see m— us? Bond Team pulling ahead in the Sherlock Shield?'

'No.' Grant ran a hand through his hair. A bad sign. 'I'm afraid I didn't see . . .' Who's dead? Jake found himself wondering. Whose parents have died? 'I'm afraid I was watching . . . something else.'

'Sir?' Cally said concernedly. 'Is anything wrong?'

'I'd like you to come with me, Bond Team.' Grant seemed to recover himself. 'A situation has arisen.'

'Situation, sir?' Ben was annoyed. What could be more important that the celebration of their victory?

'It's started,' Grant said. 'CHAOS is coming.'

EPISODE TWO:

The Chaos Connection

WRITTEN BY:

A. J. Butcher

PRODUCED BY

www.atombooks.co.uk

for Tony Joyce
The serial story started it

**PART
ONE**

ONE

The room was screaming.

To be fair, making noise was what Spy High's Intelligence Gathering Centre did. The IGC was wired into every significant news network on the planet, as well as most of the insignificant ones, monitoring events across the globe as they happened, relaying the latest developments in human history directly and immediately to the school where Jonathan Deveraux and his team of tutors could decide what action, if any, the graduates of Spy High needed to take in order to protect and preserve the good. Twenty-four hours a day, sometimes longer, the IGC echoed and re-echoed with the sound of a million voices in a thousand languages. Bond Team were used to that. They expected it.

But they didn't expect the horrors that greeted them today.

Terror and trauma on every continent. Carnage and calamity from pole to pole. Apocalyptic images like nightmares come true blazing from the screens around them. A hovertel tossed from the skies and hitting the earth like a fireball. Computer-controlled traffic colliding and exploding. The solar cities of the Californian coast plunged into darkness. And on every screen, the same the soundtrack to disaster: the whole world screaming. For once, no translation was necessary. Death has a common language.

'What's happening?' Cally stared shocked at the screens. 'It's like the end of the world.'

Lori slipped her hand into Ben's. Even though he didn't think to squeeze it reassuringly, it still felt better there.

'Sir?' A dismayed Jake turned to Grant.

'Keep watching,' the tutor instructed.

'I can't,' Jennifer protested, unusually squeamish. 'This is too . . . turn it off! Stop it now!'

The screens went dead. A second of silence, almost as disturbing as the screams. Then on every screen, multiplied and menacing, a man in a mask like a photographic negative, the reverse of a human face, and Bond Team knew why they were here.

'We have spoken,' announced the man, 'and our words have been heard in destruction, disorder and death throughout the world. Our language is CHAOS, a language your laughable so-called governments will soon come to understand more clearly than ever before. CHAOS: The Crusade for Havoc Anarchy and the Overthrow of Society. We are the enemies of your petty and repressive systems of order, your laws and your institutions.' The man in the mask leaned closer. 'Their days are numbered. Law and order will be no more. It is time for CHAOS. We have spoken and you have heard.

We will be silent now for a while, so that you may consider what has been said, but we will return with our demands. And do not think that you can stop us. We can attack anyone, anywhere, at any time. CHAOS is coming. And there is nothing you can do.'

'I don't know. We can shut this guy up for a start, can't we?' Eddie looked across the room. 'Where's the "off" switch?'

'It doesn't matter,' Grant said as the IGC went silent of its own accord for the second time. 'That was the entire communication. A little over an hour ago, it interrupted every major television broadcast worldwide. It seems this organisation is claiming responsibility for the sequence of disasters you've just witnessed. Worse, it seems to be promising more.'

'Then they've got to be stopped,' Ben said, rather obviously.

'We've already reassigned all graduate teams to this one case,' Grant said, 'and we're trying to trace the source of their signal, so far without success. Whatever masking program they're using, it must be state of the art or beyond. What we need, and quickly, is a lead.'

'Which is where you come in, Bond Team.' The videscreens were resurrected again. Now the grave, wise features of Jonathan Deveraux himself regarded the six students, examining them steadily. 'Your earlier encounter with a CHAOS agent may provide us with precisely the lead of which Senior Tutor Grant speaks.'

Bond Team exchanged glances. As one their minds drifted back to the past, last term. To their camping trip in the Wildscape. To their capture by Dr Averill

Frankenstein, the mad geneticist. And to their brief
videscreen dialogue with a similarly masked CHAOS
agent.

It was rare for Deveraux to be seen by Spy High's students, and even when he was it was only ever via a
screen, but for the founder to ask for help as explicitly as
this was unprecedented. If they could only make a contribution towards the defeat of CHAOS, Ben was
thinking, there'd need to be a special place in the Hall of
Heroes set aside just for them, with himself, as team
leader, tastefully prominent. But sadly, not even he
dared tell Deveraux anything but the discouraging truth:
'I don't think there is anything, sir, we were fully
debriefed after the event . . .'

'I am aware of that, Stanton,' said Deveraux. 'I have
the tapes.'

'Of course, sir.' Ben sounded shamed. 'I only meant
that I can't think of anything else.'

'Were you not helpless in Frankenstein's gene
chamber for much of the time? Perhaps some of your
team-mates have more to contribute.'

'Actually, sir,' said Cally, feeling that Deveraux was
being a little unfair, 'I doubt we can add any more than
Ben. The agent we saw said exactly the same kind of
things as this one today. It could even be the same man,
what with the mask and everything.'

Deveraux uttered a disappointed sigh. With it, Ben's
special place in the Hall of Heroes seemed to vanish.
'Very well. But if anything does occur to you, any of you,
no matter how slight or inconsequential it might seem to
be, bring it to the attention of Senior Tutor Grant at once.

We must explore every possible avenue in this present crisis. We cannot rest until the threat of CHAOS is over.'

Deveraux blinked out.

Stung by the founder's implicit criticism, Ben took charge. 'Meeting,' he hissed conspiratorially to the others. 'The girls' room. In an hour. Before Weapons Instruction. Let's go through the Frankenstein business again, just in case.' He was pleased to see the general nods of agreement. 'Everyone be there, right? Everyone.'

That was clear enough, Ben thought. Time. Place. Purpose. So it was a bit of a shock for him when Bond Team reconvened with one member short, and the last person he would have expected to be missing.

'Where's Lori?' he said.

She sat in the rec room but she could have been any-where. Her eyes were open but they weren't seeing her immediate environment.

Inside her head, Lori was back in Frankenstein's gene chamber.

She shuddered as she relived her ordeal. Pounding on unyielding glass. Trapped, a specimen in a jar. The gene gas itself, lapping at her ankles, rising to her knees, her thighs, a grey tide dragging at her helpless limbs. Tasting it, bitter and acrid in her mouth, when her lips had been prised open by the need to breathe. And worst of all, feeling it working on her, reshaping her, moulding some-thing new from the inside out, feeling herself drifting, her identity, her humanity drowning.

Lori squeezed her eyes shut, as if memories could be denied that way. Maybe some could, but not this one.

The gene chamber was always going to be with her, a constant and chilling reminder of her own mortality.

She'd told Ben how she felt, of course. He'd been appropriately sympathetic – all concerned expression, soothing hands and calming kisses, but it was clear he hadn't really understood. And this from someone who'd been trapped alongside her in the gene chamber, who'd tasted the transforming gas with her. The experience hadn't seemed to have affected Ben, or if it had, he wasn't letting on. *'But it's all right now, babe. It's all done with,'* he'd said. *'We survived.'* Which was true. *'The gene chamber's been destroyed.'* Also true. *'You can forget about it now.'* Well, two out of three wasn't bad.

But she didn't want to go over it all again. Let the others meet up and discuss it if they wanted to. She'd make her excuses to Ben in due course. For now, all she wanted to do was sit here quietly and not be disturbed.

Somebody else had other ideas.

'Vanessa? Vanessa, how charming of you to come.'

To begin with Lori didn't respond, largely because her name was not Vanessa. But it was hard to remain oblivious when Gadge Newbolt plumped himself down in front of her, beaming as if he was meeting an old friend for the first time in years.

Gadge Newbolt, or Professor Henry Newbolt, to be more accurate, had been the scientific genius behind virtually all of Spy High's technological marvels, hence his nickname – Gadge as in gadget.

'Vanessa,' he crooned again. Lori glanced behind her. No likely Vanessa there. 'My dear.'

Unfortunately Newbolt's brilliant brain had burned out long ago, and his famous grey cells were heaped in his skull like ashes. Now he was little more than an old man in a white coat, allowed to wander the college corridors at will as a kind of embarrassed reward for all he'd contributed in the past. Before he went senile.

Nowadays, though, Gadge tended only to talk to walls, not people. And he'd never before now, to Lori's knowledge, called anyone Vanessa.

'Professor Newbolt,' she addressed him nervously, wondering where the 'my dear' had come from. She'd been warned about old men in white coats.

'Professor ...? No, my dear,' old Gadge laughed, 'what happened to grandfather? Call me grandfather like you always used to.'

Whoops. Ben's meeting was suddenly seeming quite an attractive option, after all. 'Nice to see you, Professor, but I've got to be ...' Lori stood, smiling falsely. And saw the hurt in the old man's eyes. His thin lips quivered. 'Don't go, Vanessa,' he said. 'Not so soon. Not again. You've only just arrived, and you haven't been to see your old grandfather for such a long time.'

'Professor, I'm not Vanessa.' Lori's first thought was to put Gadge right. But then his brow furrowed, and she realised it would probably cause less harm if she pretended and played along with his delusions.

'Vanessa?' A final plaintive plea.

'Yes, grandfather?' she tried.

Gadge brightened again immediately, grasped her hands in his and shook them as Lori resumed her seat. 'Oh, it is good to see you, my dear. It's been too long.

Your old grandfather was beginning to wonder whether you'd forgotten him.'

Might be some truth there, Lori thought. She determined to find out more about Gadge's past if she could. But for now: 'Oh, no, I've been busy, that's all. Of course I'd never forget you.'

'Vanessa, Vanessa.' Gadge dabbed fat, wet tears from his eyes. 'You always were a good girl. And I've been busy, too, very busy indeed. Come and see what your old grandfather's been doing. See what I've got to show you in my lab.'

Now this was probably going too far. Gadge had hopped to his feet and was tugging eagerly at Lori's arm, and she knew she'd have to make her excuses now. Lessons resumed in a few minutes and it wasn't a good idea to skip them. Miss a class at Spy High and you could miss something that one day might save your life. She'd have to leave. But then Gadge let go of her anyway. His hands fluttered in the air like falling leaves.

'Vanessa?' he said pathetically. 'Where is my lab? I can't seem to . . . where is it?' He was like a child parted from its parents in a vast and terrifying public place. 'Vanessa, can you help me? Please help me. Take me to my lab.'

Lori sighed. How could she refuse? She'd have to catch up on her Weapons Instruction later.

'It's all right,' she said, taking the old man's hand. 'Let's go to your lab. Grandfather.'

'Grandfather?' If Ben's jaw dropped any lower, Lori would be able to inspect his tonsils from the other side of the room. 'You actually called him *grandfather*?'

'Well, yes, I didn't see why not, Ben, what else could I do?' She looked for support from Cally, who seemed keen to provide it by repeating her last words and nodding a lot – 'That's right, what else could she do?' – and from Jennifer, who was sitting glazedly on her bed and not registering any interest in the real world whatsoever.

'What else?' Ben wasn't convinced. 'You could have suggested the old boy get some therapy and then joined us at Lacey Bannon's Weapons Instruction lesson, that's what else.' Sometimes, he just didn't understand Lori. Where was her sense of duty? If only everyone was more like himself.

'Oh, Ben,' Lori sighed exasperatedly. 'It wasn't as easy as that. You didn't see what poor Gadge was like. You weren't there.'

'That's right,' Cally echoed. 'You weren't there.'

'Sounds like Gadge wasn't all there, either,' snorted Ben unsympathetically. 'So what happened then? It doesn't take an hour to get from Gadge's lab to the weapons chambers. Take a diversion to help some old ladies across the road, did you, Lori?'

'It's that caring attitude that makes me love you, Ben,' said his girlfriend. 'Actually, I couldn't get away at once. Gadge was so pleased that I was there. He wouldn't let me leave. He was like a little kid showing an adult his toys. Showed me all his latest inventions.'

'I thought he wasn't supposed to have invented anything worthwhile for years.'

'They were just boxes with wires poking out of them, bits of old batteries, circuits and lights. Nothing. Junk.

And yet he believed they were something wonderful. He wanted me to admire them. So I did. It was all a bit sad, really.'

'You're telling me. Humouring a senile old fool when you should have been with the rest of us learning something useful.'

Lori laughed ironically. 'What? How to kill people in interesting new ways?'

'Listen,' Ben reprimanded, 'when we're out on a mission, you're going to find a laser cannon a bit more of an asset than a cosy bedside manner. I doubt you're going to get too far with these CHAOS goons by calling them grandfather and smiling at them sweetly. Know what I mean?'

'Actually, I do know what you mean,' Lori said, 'which is why I left Gadge's lab as soon as I could. After a while, he became so absorbed in all his tinkering, he seemed to forget I was even there. Then as I was creeping out he noticed me again but he didn't call me Vanessa or anything. Didn't seem to recognise me at all. Just said this was a private lab and students weren't allowed in. His mind had obviously wandered off again, and so did I. Only by then Weapons Instruction was already over. Dare I ask if I missed anything important?'

'I'm afraid you did,' Ben said officiously. 'Lacey introduced us to the latest version of the stasis rifle with infra-red sights for shooting in the dark.'

'Yeah? Well, I hope you'll be very happy together.'

'Very funny,' he grunted. Certainly Cally seemed to think so. 'Let's hope you find things just as amusing in the Gun Run next week. Stasis rifles are in, and this one counts for the Shield. Or maybe you think winning that's a bit of a joke now as well, Lori. And maybe I'll just leave you to it.' How had his day come to this? It had started so well with the Wall, but since then it had fallen apart. First Deveraux, now Lori. Frowning petulantly, Ben turned to go.

'Oh, Ben, don't!' Lori called after him.

But he did. The door slammed.

'Have you ever thought about trading him in for a more mature model?' Cally wondered.

'I don't think I could.' Lori blushed. 'I don't think I'd want to. I know he can be difficult at times, and short with people, and intolerant, and seem a bit selfish . . .'

'Sorry, Lori,' interrupted Cally, 'but are you Ben's girl-friend or his analyst?'

'Only you should see him when we're alone.' Lori blushed again, proudly. 'Then you'd see a different Ben, a better Ben. He can be so gentle, so . . .'

'Yeah, well we don't want to go there, do we?' Cally laughed. 'We'll take your word for it, Lori, won't we, Jen?'

'Anyway, I think I'd better . . .' Lori gestured after Ben. 'I'd better apologise. Ben was right, really. I shouldn't have missed the lesson.'

'What? No way.' Cally shook her head in mock disbelief. 'He stormed out. You go after him now and we're talking personal humiliation. The way he spoke to you – let him come crawling back and apologise, Lori, assuming Ben Stanton's even physically capable of saying sorry. Let him know who's boss. That's what we'd do, isn't it, Jen?'

Cally and Lori seemed to realise both at the same time that Jennifer was not quite with them.
'Jennifer? Hello? Jen?'

```
IGC DATA FILE FBA 8320
  'Men like Boromov, Corbin and Pascal Z see tech-
  nology as reinforcing the divide between the
  rich and the poor, the haves and the have-nots
  of the world. They talk about techno-imperialism,
  about the technologically-advanced nations
  exploiting those countries that lack an indus-
  trial or scientific base. At the same time, this
  CHAOS organisation seems to be going even
  further, disrupting technology as a means of
  destabilising society itself. It seems clear to
  me that our entire way of life is facing a major
  crisis.' Professor Talbot went on to say . . .
```

She didn't sleep the whole of that night. She didn't dare. To close her eyes would be to dream, and to dream, on this night more than any other in the year, would be to invite the shadows in, to leave her defenceless before the tall, dark man, the man in the doorway.

So Jennifer lay on her back with her arms at her sides, like she was practising death, and stared at the ceiling as though it was the lid of a coffin.

And maybe she'd surrendered, anyway. Maybe she'd fallen asleep without realising it. With the room so black it was difficult to tell for sure whether her eyes were open or closed. She thought she must be sleeping because the doorway was suddenly before her and the man-shape in it. But perhaps she was still awake and the man who chuckled like the rattle of a cobra was no longer content to remain in her dreams, in her past, but was emerging into the here and now, keen to claim her. On this day of all days, that would be right.

It was the anniversary of the day he'd claimed her parents.

Jennifer whimpered softly in her throat, twisted the sheets in her hands, and longed for daylight.

'You all right, Jen?' Jake asked at breakfast, trying to look behind her eyes to where the truth might lie. 'I don't want to sound intrusive, but you look like you've seen a ghost.'

'Could be worse,' joked Ben. 'Could have seen Eddie in the shower.'

'Oh, very funny,' Eddie huffed. 'On the other hand, though, Jen, if you ever wanted to see me in the shower, I'm sure something could be arranged. You know, you scrub my back . . .'

'You're better off scrubbing the whole idea,' said Jake, a note of warning beneath the humour. 'If you know what I mean.'

'I'm fine anyway,' said Jennifer, not meeting anybody's eye. 'Just leave it.'

But Jake wasn't satisfied. If only Jennifer would allow him to get closer. He wanted to, she knew that, but still she kept shutting him out, like there was a closed door between them that she didn't dare to open. He decided to try again after martial arts, and if that didn't work he'd keep on trying. Jake Daly didn't give up easily.

It was kendo today, the way of the sword. Not steel swords with killing blades, of course, but the *shinai*, the bamboo blade.

Bond Team prepared themselves. They donned the protective armour, adjusting and tightening the breastplates, tugging on the padded gloves, hiding their faces behind the *men*, the masks with the steel grills.

Like bars, Jennifer found her blurred brain thinking as she fixed her *men* in place. Bars to imprison her, bars to suffocate her. She felt her breathing quicken, like she'd been running a great distance and was about to collapse. But it wasn't just the grill that was confusing her, her sight was thick and muddy too – nothing seemed clear around her. It was the lack of sleep, she realised, over many nights. She couldn't cope with it. And especially today on the anniversary.

Mr Korita, like Bond Team fully regaled in his *dogu* armour, drew them together, talked about the lesson. Jennifer wasn't following what he was saying. She glanced from side to side. Everybody looked the same, concealed with secret faces behind the bars. She couldn't tell who they were any more. She couldn't tell who she was.

Mr Korita had said something. And then they were selecting their *shinai*. The sword felt good in her gloved hands, strong, true, something to rely on.

Her mind whispered a memory. *'Mum! Dad! Don't leave me!'*

And she suddenly realised the masked people surrounding her were laughing. And they were backing away from her, leaving her alone in the centre of the gym with the little man who gave orders.

He was giving orders to her. His sword was raised in front of him. He wanted to fight her. She knew that she had to fight him and raised her own *shinai* accordingly. She wondered who he was.

Then he was at her, like lightning. Before she could even move to defend herself, striking at both sides of her torso, the impact of each blow dulled by her armour but felt nonetheless. And then, with an expert and almost invisible twist of his *shinai*, severing hers from her hand and sending it skittering across the floor.

Jennifer sensed the loss, floundered after her sword.

The others were laughing at her. Or were they? Or was it just the thudding of blood in her ears? The pounding of fist on door. She groped for her weapon. On her knees, she clutched its handle and crouched.

Towards her approached a man in a mask, wielding a weapon.

And she knew who it was. She suddenly knew. It was him, the night man, the man in the doorway. He'd come for her at last. But he couldn't have her. He wouldn't take her. She was not weak, not like her parents. She'd made herself strong. She'd show him how strong. She'd show them all.

A cry of rage and hurt and fury tearing from her throat, Jennifer leapt to her feet. Her body shook with anger and hate.

Show him? She'd kill him.

TWO

It hadn't been a good idea for Jennifer to be the one to face Mr Korita, Jake had known that from the start. Not today, not when she was behaving so strangely. But somehow it had happened anyway. It was as if their teacher was able to sniff out individual weaknesses like a bad smell, home in on them and exploit them ruthlessly. Jake supposed that that was what he was paid to do, to keep them on their toes. After all, you couldn't afford a bad day as a secret agent. A bad day could get you killed.

Talking of which . . .

He thought as soon as Jennifer was disarmed that that was the end of it. Fight over. He was wrong. Suddenly Jennifer was springing to her feet again, propelling herself towards their teacher and swinging her *shinai* directly at his head. Even Mr Korita seemed surprised. For a second he paused. For less than a second. Then he whipped up his own *shinai* to block Jennifer's blow. The crack of bamboo made Bond Team flinch.

Jennifer was not deterred. She struck down at his side, savagely, intending harm. Mr Korita blocked again. She whirled and aimed at his back, her *shinai* slicing open wounds in the air. Mr Korita pivoted so that the flailing sword missed him, though not by much. He tried to move to the offensive himself, but recklessly, relentlessly, Jennifer lashed blows at him, heedless of her own safety, forcing block after desperate block, pushing the teacher back.

'She's doing really well,' Ben approved.

'No, this isn't good.' Jake saw his anxiety reflected in Cally and Lori. 'She's lost it or something. This is for real.'

'What do you mean?' Eddie was with Ben. 'This is great. Sure Jen's name isn't Lee rather than Chen?'

'Shut up, Eddie,' snapped Jake. 'Open your eyes. This has got to be stopped before someone gets hurt.'

Mr Korita seemed to share a similar sentiment. They heard him call '*Yame!*' – stop – and '*Shobu-ari*' – end of contest – but Jennifer either couldn't hear or wasn't listening. Her whirling assault continued, battering the teacher's *shinai*, threatening to overwhelm him.

Mr Korita seemed to stumble, dropped to one knee.

Jennifer shouted in triumph, lifted her weapon high like an executioner's axe. Her victim's head was bowing before her.

'Jen, no!' Jake cried.

The teacher's *shinai* stabbed out, rammed Jennifer's abdomen. The blow drove home, even through her armour, like a dagger in the guts. All of a sudden, the spell was over. Jennifer was clutching at her stomach, gasping, doubling up, keeling over, her weapon clattering to the floor. Then she was on her knees, retching and shuddering, and Mr Korita was beside her, loosening the cords of her mask, removing it. Her black hair spilled like ink.

'I'm sorry,' she was panting. 'I'm so sorry.'

'Not now,' calmed Mr Korita. 'Just breathe. Slowly, deeply. You're all right.'

No, thought Jake, as Bond Team closed ranks around their fallen comrade, she isn't.

He was still thinking the same later as he stood banging on her door, knowing that she was inside, demanding that she talk to him. 'Jennifer! Jen! You can't keep this door locked forever. You've got to come out sometime. Listen, I don't know what the matter is but silence won't solve it. Let me help you. Let me in.'

Inside, curled like a foetus on her bed, Jennifer heard Jake's pleas but did not respond. Dared not. She had to be strong, for herself, for her parents. She'd been weak today in Korita's class, had let the anniversary take over and cloud her judgement, betray her inner rage. She couldn't allow that to happen again. She wouldn't.

Stone. Cold stone. That was what she had to be. Be stone, learn from Spy High, and wait for the moment that would inevitably come, and for real, not in dreams.

Yet something in Jake's voice was tempting. 'I want to help Jennifer, that's all.' She could take refuge in that. But to rely on someone else was to be vulnerable to someone else, and vulnerability was weakness. Besides, how could Jake help her? To help you had to understand, and how could Jake understand?

But when the knocking stopped and with a sigh Jake's voice drifted away, Jennifer did not feel better. It shocked her to realise that she felt worse.

'Well how much longer is he going to be?' Ben complained, tapping his watch for no apparent reason. 'We'll all have graduated before Daly gets here at this rate. I say we start now and Jake'll just have to play catch up.'

'We can't do that, Ben,' said Cally. 'Jake's gone to see whether he can get any sense out of Jennifer now, and seeing as she's the subject of our little gathering, our little gathering behind her back if I might just stress that small fact, then I think we need to wait for him.'

'You think that, do you?' said Ben. Other than Jennifer and Jake, the other members of Bond Team were grouped around a table in the quietest corner of the rec room. 'Who else thinks that?'

'Probably all of us, O leader,' said Eddie, pointing towards the door, 'particularly as here he comes now.'

'Are you all right, Jake?' asked Lori as their team-mate slumped into a seat alongside them. 'Did you talk to Jennifer?'

'Through the door,' Jake said, 'which she wouldn't open.' He shrugged with a dejected helplessness. 'I don't know what to do.'

'Well that's why we're here, isn't it?' Ben pressed. 'To decide what to do.'

'That's why *you* called us here, Ben,' corrected Cally, as if the rewording made a difference, 'though I'm not sure it's our place to *decide*, as you so cheerfully put it, about Jen or any other of our team-mates.'

'Say that again on a mission,' Ben responded, 'when Jennifer loses it Big Time like she did this morning and puts everyone's lives in jeopardy.'

'Yeah, it'd make me feel a lot better in my final moments to have you whispering "I told you so" in my ear, Benny boy.' Eddie smiled thinly.

'The point is,' Cally frowned, 'that we're not on a mission yet, and not going to be for another eighteen months at least. The point is we're still training, and part of the purpose of training is to identify and rectify any areas of weakness that we might have. Even you, Ben. See, I don't really understand why we're having this little meeting at all. Jennifer's got something she just needs to work out, that's all.'

'That's not all,' denied Ben, 'and you know it, Cally. She went wild in a normal, routine martial arts lesson. No extra psychological pressure, nothing. And there she is, trying to smash Korita's head in. That's not all. And I bet if this was happening to certain other members of the team you wouldn't be quite so vigorous in their support.'

'What's that supposed to mean?' Cally's voice rose in anger.

'Seconds away, round one,' contributed Eddie.

'Let's not get personal,' intervened Lori. 'Let's just calm down. Cally, Ben, nobody's meaning anything. We're all on the same side, remember? We all want what's best for Jen.'

'Good, Lori,' Jake approved. 'A sensible voice at last. And don't stop there. Say something else.'

'Well,' casting a slightly nervous glance towards her boyfriend, 'I have to agree with Ben. Jennifer's actions today in the kendo . . . and it's not just today either, is it? She's been increasingly, well . . . strange, self-absorbed, for a while now, hasn't she? I do think it's an issue.'

'Well, if she wants lessons in developing a warm, winning personality,' Eddie offered, 'I'm always available. Very cheap rates.'

'We want to help Jen, not doom her,' Jake said. 'Go on, Lori.'

'Well, it seems to me we have a choice. Which is why Ben called us together here in the first place, isn't it?' Ben acknowledged Lori's correctness. 'Cally's obviously right about our training, but none of the staff are with us all the time, nobody here knows Jen as well as we do. We're her team-mates, her friends. We can see there's a problem and its extent better than our teachers, even after today.'

'Agreed so far,' said Jake, and even Cally nodded, though reluctantly. 'So the choice . . .?'

'Is whether we try to deal with it among ourselves – support and help Jen within the team – or whether we report our concerns to Senior Tutor Grant.'

'But anything could happen then,' warned Cally. 'She could even be removed from the course, and you know what that means – mind-wiped and returned home like she'd never been here in the first place. No memory of us at all! I don't want that on my conscience. That's not an option.'

'This isn't about your conscience, Cally,' Ben contended, 'and as far as I'm concerned, informing Grant is the only option. And don't look at me like that. I've got nothing against Jennifer personally. I like her as much as any of you. But the fact remains that if she's unstable –'

'Unstable?' Eddie queried. 'How'd you get to that, Dr Stanton?'

'All right, if she's *unpredictable* – better?' Ben rephrased. Eddie nodded better. 'If she's unpredictable she could endanger us all. None of you can deny that.' Four pairs of eyes increasingly cast downwards suggested that Ben might be right. 'Cally's point about not being on missions yet, well we weren't planning on getting involved with Frankenstein, were we? But we did. And who knows what might happen with CHAOS now? And even if nothing does, just our day to day lessons contain risks, don't they? This isn't exactly a normal school, is it? And don't we want to win the Sherlock Shield? We have to be able to rely on each other, and if Jennifer's going to be a liability, then—'

'All right, Ben,' Jake interrupted. 'That's enough. I think we know where you stand but you're not the only one here and I think whatever we do has to be unanimous.'

Everybody agreed, though not everybody seemed to like it.

Jake continued: 'In the long term, Ben's got to be right, even though I don't like to admit it. There might come a time when the best thing for Jen will be some kind of professional help, counselling, I don't know what. But that time isn't yet, no way is it yet.' Murmurs of agreement from three of the four listeners. 'And I think it's our responsibility to help Jennifer through whatever's troubling her now, to give her our total support, and our loyalty, and our . . . friendship. And if we do that, then I think everything'll be fine and that's what I'm voting for. What about the rest of you?'

'Absolutely.' Cally.

'Yes. Yes.' Lori.

'Excuse me while I get my hanky, but yes. Agreed.' Eddie.

'It seems everybody's made their minds up. I won't rock the boat, but . . .' Ben.

'It's all right,' Eddie whispered to him. 'There's always "I told you so".'

Ben caught up with Jake later, just the two of them. It meant that neither had to pretend to like the other. Already the brief sense of unity that the boys had shared during the Frankenstein episode seemed to belong to an unlikely past.

'You were very eloquent in there,' Ben sneered. 'Could almost forget you were a Domer.'

'Your point? I don't want to keep you from your mirror.'

'My point is what you didn't say, why you really want to keep Jennifer on the team.' Ben was delighted to see Jake frown defensively. 'Unrequited love is such a pain, isn't it? Well, maybe you'll get somewhere now Jen's got to be grateful.'

Jake regarded Ben with something close to contempt. 'You really are low, aren't you, Stanton? If only Lori knew . . .'

'Lori and me are for real,' Ben returned. 'We're a real couple. We hold hands in public and everything. What about you and Jennifer, hey, Jakey? And let me tell you, it's not going to be my girl that lets the team down, you understand me? And when that happens, Jake, when Jennifer flips again, it'll be your fault, yeah? Yours.'

IGC DATA FILE FBA 8328

. . . latest in a series of raids on former asso-
ciates and haunts of known techno-terrorists. A
government spokesperson said that the operation
had been a success, recovering material of
crucial significance in the hunt for CHAOS. The
precise nature of the material was not disclosed
for reasons of national security.

'You folks can sleep safely in your beds,'
the spokesperson declared. 'Our boys are on the
case and nothing bad is gonna happen.'

Rumours continue that the President, the
Vice-President and the Joint Chiefs of Staff
have already been moved to a secret underground
base . . .

THREE

A normal day on a normal street, Lori reflected. That's what it looked like. A mother with her baby in a pram. A group of friends laughing and joking on the corner. A young couple window-shopping, their backs to the world.

No traffic, though, neither parked nor passing, which was unusual. And she herself didn't normally walk in the middle of the road. She didn't normally carry a stasis rifle, either.

But today was going to be something of an exception.

From nowhere and everywhere, a buzzer sounded. Lori tensed for action. It was her turn at the Gun Run. On screen in the control room, the others would be watching. The clock would be ticking. The honour of Bond Team was at stake.

The young couple turned to face her. Seemed they'd already made a pair of purchases. They were pointing them at Lori right now, taking aim, fingers on the trigger.

No trouble. Too slow. Lori was firing the stasis rifle almost before the threat was established. The stasis bolts jolted into the forms of her attackers. They snapped open silent mouths, jerked with contortions as a shimmering blue light rippled through them, finally stiffened, and fell. The paralysis effect of the stasis bolts was virtually immediate.

Which was just as well. Lori whirled in a new direction. The group of friends were no longer laughing and joking, no longer on the corner. They'd spread out across the street and were running towards her, blazing at her with shock pistols, the shells ripping at the road around her.

This was more challenging. Multiple targets and at a distance from each other. Her aim had to be faultless. Luckily for Lori, false modesty aside, it pretty much was. She eliminated the nearest assailant first – always the priority – the stasis bolts slamming him backwards. Lori went down on one knee. Second priority: make yourself a smaller target. She fired again and again, not wasting a single shot. They'd be cheering her in the control room, she knew. Ben would be working out whether her time was likely to be good enough to beat Simon Macey and Solo Team. At this rate, she thought, as her final attacker crashed to the ground, he could start popping the champagne corks – if alcohol hadn't been banned at Spy High.

Lori was on her feet again. The street was clear and she could . . . not take anything for granted. A tell-tale click to her left. The mother. The unexpected. Leaving baby in the pram while she fired a shock pistol at Lori's head. Lori dived forward, firing her own weapon as she did. Mother spasmed as the bolts shocked her system. Surely she was safe now, Lori was thinking.

But there was one final surprise. The killers on the Gun Run started early. Baby sat up. Baby was armed and dangerous in her pram. It was a difficult shot, but Lori struck the forehead just beneath the bonnet.

Baby's mouth snapped open as the others' mouths had done, and made an equal amount of silence. Because baby, like the others, was an animate, a robot, part of the program.

Only Lori was real, Lori and the pressure of time.

She raced for the door at the end of the street. Her daylight Run was over. Now she had to do it in the dark.

Through the door it was sudden night. Pitch black. Only a faint luminous glow on the floor, something like Spy High's answer to the Yellow Brick Road, showed Lori the way to go. This was no longer an environment where a successful secret agent wanted to rely solely on her own sight. Lori switched to radar vision, yanking the specially treated film from her belt and wrapping it round her eyes. It clicked into place. Now she had eyes not only in the back of her head but along its entire circumference. Lori was seeing the circle.

And just in time. A dangerous shape materialized behind her and to the right. Lori dropped to one knee again, fired the stasis rifle.

Missed. She frowned in disbelief. *Missed?*

She fired again. Got him, but not fatally. Her aim wasn't quite as sure in the dark and the clock was ticking. The third time her attacker fell, but behind her another two were approaching, already shooting at her. The air around crackled and sparked.

Lori rolled over on the floor, stasis bolts stabbing at her assailants' legs. They went down but she was wasting time, losing time. Her heart thudded an anxious warning. What had Ben said, about the weapons instruction lesson she'd missed? (As further enemies intruded between her and the way out.) 'Lacey introduced us to the latest version of the stasis rifle.' (As she fired. And missed. And fired.) 'With infra-red sights for shooting in the dark.' (And missed again.)

She didn't know how to do it. How did you activate the infra-red sights?

Her assailants were advancing. They were taking aim. She'd given them too much time.

In the control room, they wouldn't be cheering now. Lori could imagine Ben's face. Aghast. And what had she said to him? 'Yeah? Well, I hope you'll be very happy together.' Maybe in future she'd better leave the sarcasm to Eddie.

Lori fumbled with her stasis rifle. It wasn't going to do her any good. She heard her attackers fire.

And she died. Ben was *not* going to be pleased.

She was right. He wasn't. It was little short of a miracle that Ben managed to restrain his fury with her for as long as he did, while the others commiserated and claimed she was unlucky, and that it wouldn't make any difference anyway in the long run – Bond Team were still too good to be beaten to the Shield by Macey and his mates. But Lori could tell from Ben's purpling face, like he was secretly being boiled, that he didn't entirely agree. 'Can we talk, Lori?' he mumbled, hardly trusting himself to part his lips. 'Just you and me. In an empty classroom, maybe.'

When it came Ben's eruption would have buried a town three times the size of Pompeii. 'What did you think you were playing at? Do you know what you've done, Lori?'

'I'm sorry, Ben.' She hung her head in shame, knowing he was right.

'Sorry's just a word,' Ben hurled back. 'A word that losers use. And you know what, babe? You might just have single-handedly turned us into losers. Look at the scores now. Macey's lot and us – neck and neck. Two events left. If you'd have pulled your weight in the Gun Run we'd have been well ahead.'

'I know it's my fault, Ben,' Lori admitted abjectly. She couldn't bear him glaring at her. She felt like a little girl scolded. She remembered how frightened she'd used to be at a single harsh word from her father.

'You bet your baby blues it's your fault, Lo,' Ben scolded. 'That's why I'm mad. You were off Good Samaritaning with senile old Gadge when you should have been learning how to infra-red the stasis rifle with us. You clearly didn't bother to catch up in your own time so you get frazzled on your Gun Run and lose us vital points.'

'Ben . . . please . . .' But Lori could deny none of it.

'So what's going on, Lori? You on Simon Macey's side now, is that it?'

'No, of course not.' Lori was shocked. 'How can you say that? How can you even think . . .?' She put out her arms to Ben.

He stepped backwards with disdain, like a rich man to a beggar. 'I don't want to touch you right now, Lori,' he said coldly. 'Right now, I'm not even sure I want to look at you. You've let me down, you realise that? I can't . . .' A look of genuine pain scarred Ben's features. 'You've let me down.'

He turned on his heel and stalked from the room. His anger must have made him deaf. He didn't respond to a single one of Lori's pleas for him to stay and for them to talk it through. His rage must have blinded him, too. He never noticed Simon Macey lurking outside the class-room, greedily devouring every syllable that had passed between him and Lori.

Simon smiled to himself, and nodded knowingly. He gazed at an unhappy Lori through the glass of the class-room door. And planned.

```
IGC DATA FILE FBA 8330
   . . . unexpected consumer boom in the wake of the
   CHAOS atrocities.
     'What's the point of saving for a rainy day
   now?' demanded one frantic shopper. 'If CHAOS
   has its way, there probably aren't many days
   left. Me, I'm going to have a heck of a good
   time before the lights go out.'
```

Jennifer crouched in the bushes close to the athletics track and watched Jake running. He'd already completed several laps, his singlet hanging with increasing dampness from him, but he didn't look like he was anywhere near ready to stop. His expression was stony and set, his limbs on automatic. He was chasing something that he couldn't catch.

Part of Jennifer was enjoying her secret spectatorship, was admiring the strength of Jake's body, the power of his pounding legs. Part of her was. Another part of her was wondering what on earth she was doing, skulking about in the undergrowth like some sort of Peeping Tom. Why wasn't she in the holo-gym if she was feeling a little more balanced again, practising her kendo, her judo, her karate, her anything that allowed her to hit people on one of the combat programs? Or why, if she was feeling better, wasn't she apologising to the others for her recent behaviour?

Because Jake wasn't in the holo-gym, that was why, or with the others. Jake was here. If only she could find the courage to approach him.

It might have helped Jennifer if real people could sprout thought balloons above their heads, like characters in comic books. Then she'd have realised that there was only one subject in Jake's mind, and that was her.

He'd thought maybe a good long run would relax him, or help him find answers to the question of Jennifer Chen. Neither had happened. Why couldn't it be easy, Jake wondered? Why couldn't he have fallen for Cally when she'd revealed her feelings for him before Christmas? Or why couldn't Jennifer be as frank and as open as Lori? Why did not having a girlfriend, not having Jen, make him feel annoyingly inferior to Romeo

Stanton? Basically, Jake mused mournfully, why wasn't he very good with girls?

The pitifulness of his position suddenly made him want to laugh. He did. He gazed up at the sky, like an endless blue field, and laughed out loud. The existence of the sky always made him feel better. This sky, anyway – the free, unfiltered sky, the sky outside of the domes. Okay, Jake reasoned, so he had a bit of a problem with Jen, but things could be worse. He could still be back in Dome Thirteen, Oklahoma State, imprisoned there by a ceiling of glass. Count your blessings, his old gran had told him. All right, then: *One*.

Jake slowed to a jog, then a stop. Cally and Eddie were rushing towards him from the college building, calling his name, waving. There was an urgency in Cally's voice, a note of warning that chilled the sweat on Jake's back and made him tremble with more than exertion. For the second time recently, Jake found himself wondering: who's died? Whose parents have died and his friends come to tell him?

'Oh, Jake, Jake.' Cally was distraught. 'We've just heard. In the IGC. Something terrible's happened.'

'What is it, Cal?' Jake gripped her shoulder. 'Tell me.'

Even from her distance, Jennifer could sense grave news, even though she couldn't hear her team-mates' words. But she was excluded from it. She couldn't go to him now. She couldn't just get up and saunter across the athletics track. She squatted in the bushes, alone and ashamed.

'There's been another attack,' Eddie said, as Cally's voice failed her. 'Another CHAOS attack, Jake.' And it was Eddie's seriousness that disturbed him most, made Eddie almost unrecognisable, and the moment unreal, 'Jake, they've brought down a dome.'

'They've brought down a dome.' Not unreal. It had been done. 'Which one?' An unnecessary question, but he repeated it anyway. 'Which one?'

Cally's eyes brimmed with tears. The single, fateful word. 'Yours.'

FOUR

That morning, Beth took Peggy and Glubb to the far field. It was a kind of treat because Peggy and Glubb had been such good dolls lately and Beth had promised to show them the world. You could see just about the whole world from the far field. There it was, stretching off in every direction as far as the eye could see, the boundless expanse of wheat like a tranquil yellow sea and the distant farm houses bobbing upon it like ships with walls for sails.

The world was a bit much for Peggy and Glubb who started to cry. They could no longer see their home and everything was a bit too big and they were very small. Beth didn't mind them crying. She hugged and kissed them and it made her feel better. 'You mustn't be frightened,' she told them. 'Our world is just the dome, but outside the dome there's another world with cities in it and so many people you couldn't possibly count them and they all talk at once and that's where Jake's gone.'

She thought of her big brother a lot. It made her sad sometimes when she remembered him leaving – the rows like fights between him and Ma and Pa, who didn't want him to go. Where had he gone? A school somewhere, Beth thought. Why all the fuss about going to school? But she remembered Jake's final kiss and how Pa would not walk with him to the bus, and how she watched her brother go on his way and grow small and then vanish among the timeless fields. She remembered it and she sobbed.

Now it was Peggy and Glubb's turn to console her. 'Don't cry,' they said, even though they were made of rags and not fancy animate-dolls like those Beth had seen in the shop windows at the Border Zone. 'One day Jake will come back,' they said, even though they had no mouths. 'One day he'll come back and you'll be together again.'

Of course he would. Jake had said so, hadn't he? He wouldn't leave his little sister forever. Beth cuddled her dolls gratefully, Peggy who was pretty enough, even without a mouth, to be a model one day, and Glubb who, well . . . modelling wasn't for everyone, was it?

All three of them lay back and gazed at the sky and the ceiling above the sky, the glittering steel arches and winking glass panels of the dome. Peggy and Glubb trembled. Beth laughed. 'It's nothing to be scared of, the dome,' she reassured them. Though she remembered her own baby fears, that the criss-cross pattern above her was nothing more or less than a giant spider's web, and that she and Ma and Pa and Jake were all like flies caught in it, and that somewhere there must be the spider who spun the web, and that one day (or probably night) he would return to claim them all.

But of course, that was childish nonsense. Her Pa had said so. He'd said that the dome was there to protect them, to keep them safe and warm and comfortable, and that it made the soil rich and the crops grow. The dome was good, her Pa had said. So Beth was friends with it now, and told Peggy and Glubb the same thing.

'The dome will always be there,' she told them.

The steel struts above her shuddered, as with sudden fear. The glass panels tensed like staring eyes.

'The dome is good to us. The dome looks after us. The dome is our friend.'

The dome quivered and Beth gasped. Bolts of crackling energy, that if the little girl had ever seen a storm she'd probably have thought of as lightning, surged along the steel arches of the structure, coiled around them like fingers, like fists. Pulled. With immeasureable, irresistible power.

Pulled apart.

The dome squealed its agony. It found an echo in Beth who was on her feet now and screaming at the sky. Her little heart frozen inside her.

She could see something beyond the glass, something dark and evil lurking. Something that knew nothing but death. And she knew, in one blinding, blistering moment of horror, that she'd been right all along.

She didn't have time to dwell on it. With a grinding, wrenching groan that made the earth shake, the steel arches ruptured. The sky split open in deep, gashing wounds. Panels of glass shattered and fell like icebergs. A downpour at last had come to the dome.

Too terrified now even to scream, Beth fled for her home. Too terrified now even to think. Peggy and Glubb remained in the field, to fend for themselves as best they could. There was room now in Beth's astounded mind for one idea only.

The sky was falling.

IGC DATA FILE FBA 8345

. . . but by then it was too late. Further evacuation was impossible, and the people of the dome were forced to fend for themselves, farmers and their families cut off from the outside world, huddling together beneath what shelter they could find and hoping and praying that they would survive the disaster's deadly debris.

Emergency services from across the state are now on the scene and the remaining domes have been evacuated in case of further attacks. The final death toll may not be known for many days, while hospitals in the surrounding area are already stretched to capacity and beyond . . .

They didn't let Jake anywhere near the IGC. For him to see the dome's destruction magnified a hundred times on a hundred screens amid the clamour of a thousand shouting voices, would not have been a good idea. Cally and Lori doubted that it was advisable for Jake to watch the news footage at all, but he fixed them with a look of such pain and passion and pride that they knew they couldn't, wouldn't stand in his way. Jake needed to witness the disaster for himself.

After all, the dome had been his home.

And it was bad. They were with Jake in the boys' room, all of Bond Team. It was on the TV, of course, every channel, the same footage repeated like an endless loop of tragedy. Jake hadn't even changed from his run. He didn't care what he was wearing. He was scouring the screen hungrily, desperately. There was a wild, mad hope in him that he might see his Ma or Pa or little Beth among the survivors, wrapped up in blankets and being administered a hot drink by a caring, in-control member of the emergency services. He needed a sign that they were safe.

Ben didn't think he'd get one, but he didn't dare say so. It was still too soon after the event for casualties to be recorded. He looked at the screen. The dome was like a smashed eggshell, the fertile land inside splintered with giant and jagged shards of glass, sliced open, and gouged with colossal, twisted girders, farms and settlements buried beneath. It was carnage, Ben reflected darkly. It was chaos.

And he felt ashamed. How many times had he ridiculed Jake because of his background, had called him a Domer as a term of abuse or belittlement? Too many times, and each one was now returning to haunt him. Who was he to dismiss and look down on people just because they worked the land and were poor while his own father owned whole buildings and was rich? And now, many of those same people he'd scorned and mocked were dead or had suffered their livelihoods' ruin.

These were people he was supposed to be training to protect.

Ben couldn't endure the screen any longer. He turned to his team-mates instead. Cally and Lori were on either side of the distraught Jake, holding and squeezing one hand each, comforting him with meaningless sounds. Lori was very close to Jake but for once Ben could not bring himself to mind. Eddie, his one-liners silenced by events, hovered uncomfortably by the door. Jennifer hunched dismally on a bed, glancing at Jake from time to time with a strange, half-longing, half-fearful expression, but she said nothing either.

Then Jake was on his feet, pointing, crying out: 'I know that farm! That's old Frank Sanders' place. It looks . . . is he . . .? We live . . . ours is the next farm . . .' He shook off the girls' hands. 'I'm going. I've got to go there. They need me. My family need me. I've got to help them.'

Jennifer quietly began to cry. Nobody really noticed.

Attention was fixed on Jake who was striding for the door. 'Jake, wait!' Cally called. 'Someone, don't let him go!'

Ben stepped between Jake and the door. Eddie faded away.

'You're in my way, Stanton,' Jake growled. 'Get out of it or I'll make you get out of it, and you don't want that to happen, believe me.'

Ben saw the danger in Jake's eyes. What he said was going to be crucial. 'Listen to me, Jake.' Trust me, he thought, though without much hope. 'You can't just go. I can't let you. Not in your present . . . you leave the college without permission, that's immediate expulsion, you know that.'

'Listen to him, Jake.' Several voices together.

'I don't care.' Anger, hurt, frustration in Jake's tone, the feelings that cannot be controlled. 'How can I care about anything when my family could be . . .' He pushed Ben hard with the flat of his hand. 'Stanton, I'm warning you.'

'No, Jake, listen. Grant's checking about your family. He'll find out what's happened. Soon. Before anything official. You've got to wait. You've got to stay here.'

'Ben's right, Jake,' said Lori, stroking his shoulders.

'What's your game, Stanton?' Jake was suddenly suspicious. 'What do you care?'

It was a chance for Ben, a chance to say he did care, to apologise, to perhaps put things right between himself and Jake.

Senior Tutor Grant entered the room. His face was as grey as his hair.

Silence. Instant. Absolute.

'Sir?' breathed Jake.

Grant returned his gaze. 'I have some news . . .'

Half an hour earlier, Grant had been sitting uncomfortably in the rooms of Jonathan Deveraux himself, rooms where entry was not allowed without the founder's specific permission. The Senior Tutor was running his hands through his hair almost obsessively, but Deveraux did not appear to notice. These days, there were many small but telling things he didn't seem to notice.

The CHAOS agent on the videscreen was not one of them. 'We have spoken again,' the negative mask intoned. It could have been the same man as before; it could have been another. 'And our voice has shattered a dome. CHAOS has come to your quiet states, America. CHAOS walks your fields and withers your crops. Out of plenty, CHAOS can bring hunger. We could smash every one of your much-vaunted domes if we so choose, break them like eggs. But we have decided not to do so.'

'Why the sudden generosity?' grumbled Grant. 'Don't tell me they've found God all of a sudden.'

'Their demands,' said Deveraux.

'Our demands,' said the agent. 'The Crusade for Havoc Anarchy and the Overthrow of Society is offended by the ridiculous institutions in the world that have come to be called governments – those futile bodies of men and women who seek for their own ends to restrict and restrain the wider impulses of the people by passing what are laughably known by the oppressed of the globe as laws. The Crusade for Havoc Anarchy and the Overthrow of Society rejects laws. We repudiate law-makers. Therefore we demand the resignation of every so-called government on the planet within the time scale of one week. If the world can be created in seven days, then CHAOS can reshape it in the same period. And be warned, the consequences of disobedience will be severe. Further domes await destruction if our ultimatum is not met. For we are CHAOS, and—'

'Is there much more of this, sir?' hinted Grant.

'Only more of the same,' said Deveraux, 'and we don't need to hear it.' The CHAOS agent's grinning mask blinked into blankness. 'In any case, I would sooner hear about Jake Daly.'

'We're obviously doing what we can to find out about his family. His team-mates are with him at the moment, I understand, but he's taking it hard. Who wouldn't?'

'Of course, of course,' Deveraux said, thoughtfully rather than with concern, as if he might number himself among the wouldn'ts.

'At least they've made demands now, sir.' Grant tried to redirect the conversation. 'Impossible to meet, of course, but with a second contact, too, we might be able to delay the deadline by negotiations while a team tracks CHAOS down.' A pause, as if Deveraux hadn't heard. 'Sir?'

'We can use this calamity to our advantage, Grant,' the founder said at last.

'Sir?'

'Whether the Dalys are dead or alive, Jake will want to go home, won't he?'

Grant was baffled. What had the possible bereavement of one of his students to do with anything? Sometimes these days, Deveraux disturbed him.

'Ah, and it seems there is important information on this matter coming through now . . .'

'They're alive?' Though it was what Jake wanted to hear, it was more than he'd dared to believe. 'They're alive? And my sister, too?'

'All of them,' Grant said. 'Safe and well. It's true.'

'They're alive.' Jake was laughing, crying, nodding inanely to his team-mates, who clustered round with congratulations. Except Ben, who kept at a distance so as not to risk a charge of hypocrisy. Except Jennifer, who seemed lost in sorrows of her own.

'I'm so glad,' Lori said, flinging her arms tightly around Jake's shaking form. 'We're all so glad for you, Jake.'

'There's one thing more.' Grant turned away from Jake almost guiltily, faced Ben instead. 'Mr Deveraux has given Jake three days leave to return home, to be with his parents and give what help he can.'

'Thank you,' Jake said, voice thick with emotion. 'Thank Mr Deveraux.'

'And he wants a team to go with Jake,' Grant added. 'Ben, you as team leader, naturally, and two others. Those who don't go will stay at the college to retain a Bond Team presence.'

'But why . . .?' Ben didn't entirely understand.

'Support for Jake, first of all,' Grant said quickly, 'but also, Mr Deveraux thinks it'll give you a chance to look around and, perhaps, given your brief association with CHAOS, find some kind of clue, some kind of lead.'

Ben stiffened. So Deveraux was calling on him after all. He felt pride returning, so much more palatable an emotion than shame. He thought of the Hall of Heroes and himself immortalised in it. 'Of course,' he announced. 'We'll do whatever the founder wants.'

'I expected nothing less,' said Grant, with the slightest and wryest of smiles. 'Pick your team. You leave tonight.'

'Cally,' selected Ben. 'We might need your computer skills.' Cally nodded, embraced Jake. 'And . . .' Ben glanced between Eddie, Jennifer and Lori. He could leave Eddie, of course. He'd not even been at Frankenstein's lodge when they'd encountered the first CHAOS agent. Eddie couldn't contribute. So it was a straight choice between Jennifer and Lori. No choice at all, then. Either Jennifer, who just the other day he'd been advocating ought to be removed from the team for psychological counselling, or Lori, his girlfriend, who last term had finished in close second place to him in all tests and examinations.

No, for Ben there was no choice at all.

Her first reaction was that she'd misheard. Jennifer. Lori. They sounded about the same, didn't they? You could easily get them confused, couldn't you? That was it. The name Ben had spoken, his final selection, had only sounded like Jennifer. In fact he'd said Lori. It stood to reason, didn't it? Well, actually, no. Jennifer, sadly, bafflingly for Lori, pretty much always meant Jennifer. Ben had picked Jen instead of her.

He'd picked Jen ahead of her.

Second reaction – later and alone together, when Ben was preparing for departure – 'Why, Ben? I mean, I know you're team leader and everything, and it's not really my place to question your decisions on matters like this, but, well, what you were saying about Jen's unpredictability . . .' She was thinking Gun Run. She couldn't help it.

'What the rest of you were saying about giving her our total support,' responded Ben. 'This could be just what Jennifer needs, take her out of school for a while, out of herself, maybe.' But he couldn't meet Lori's gaze, the hurt in her eyes. Ben was thinking of the Gun Run, too, and of his motives. He was already beginning to regret them. That annoying sense of shame was hanging around again, like a policeman on his beat.

'Well,' said Lori cautiously, 'if that's the only reason . . .'

'What other reason could there be?' Keeping the defensiveness to a minimum. Promising himself to make it up to Lori when he got back. 'And, Lori, listen, another thing. I wanted you to stay here 'cause I need someone to keep an eye on Simon Macey, just in case he tries something to steal a lead over us in the Sherlock Shield. You know? I need someone I can trust, Lori. That's you.'

She brightened then. Ben needed someone he could trust. That was her. She'd been wrong to doubt him. He'd obviously forgiven her misdemeanour in the Gun Run. She'd still have preferred to be going to the dome of course, but she'd be professional and make the best of it. Ben was relying on her.

So she went to see the others off that evening in good heart, and with a special hug for Jake. 'Look after yourself,' she urged. 'I'll be thinking of you.'

'Okay, let's go,' Ben hurried. 'We'll keep in touch, let you know what's happening.'

'Excellent,' Eddie said. 'We'll look forward to that, won't we, Lori?'

There were further hugs, waves, goodbyes. Two thirds of Bond Team departed for the dome. One third was left in the gathering darkness in the courtyard outside Deveraux's main entrance.

Eddie nudged Lori. 'Guess we're officially the B team

now, what do you think? It's good to know your place in the world, wouldn't you say, Lori? Hey, I've got an idea, though. We could always look for consolation and start a mad passionate affair together, couldn't we? I'm willing to give it a go if you are.'

'Eddie,' Lori couldn't help but smile, 'in your dreams.'

'Really? I'd better get to bed, then, right away. You coming? Inside, I mean.'

'Why not?' Lori sighed. 'Nothing to stay out here for.' She turned towards the school.

Simon Macey was leaning against the door. He was staring directly at her. Just for a moment she saw him. Then he was gone.

'Eddie, did you see Simon . . .?'

'Who? No. I think my sight's still a bit blurry after that tearful departure. I think you might have to lead me to my room.'

'I think you might have to get used to disappointment.'

Lori was puzzled, unsettled. Keep an eye on Simon Macey, Ben had said. Well, it seemed that Simon Macey was keeping an eye on her.

FIVE

IGC DATA FILE FBA 8350

. . . against accusations of complacency regarding the threat from CHAOS ahead of this latest
atrocity. Amid heckling and jeers, the press
officer admitted that no positive leads towards
identifying CHAOS bases had yet been secured,
but he stressed that all the resources at the
administration's disposal were being brought to
bear on the crisis and that progress would only
be a matter of time. The government, he added,
to cries of 'shame,' would not be resigning.

And so, while politicians prattle and the
military muddles, the world is left to watch and
wait, and hope that someone somewhere knows what
they are doing . . .

At the Border Zone, the four members of Bond Team
mounted the SkyBikes that were waiting for them and
headed towards the Daly farm without delay. Just the

day before yesterday, this would doubtlessly have been a
most pleasant journey, the warmth of the perfectly controlled temperature relaxing the body, the slightest of
artificial breezes rippling across the fields, the very air
itself filtered and purified. And circling the traveller to
the limits of the vision, good land rich and abundant with
crops, a land at peace with itself. But the day before yesterday was no longer, and the land was scoured by the
dome's deadly debris. Rain drizzled from the darkness of
the sky, wild rain, untamed by science, and there was no
defence against it.

The wide, open spaces made Cally nervous, more
nervous even than the hunks of metal that jabbed from
the ground where they had plunged, like masterpieces of
abstract art. Cally had been born and bred in the city.
She liked walls, she liked streets, she liked the pressure
of people and things around her. Out here among the
domes, it was too easy to get lost. She hoped they'd reach
Jake's soon and that the farm was still standing. She
wanted to get inside and shut a door.

Ben wasn't warming to the dome, either, but for different reasons from Cally. The place was so narrow, so
limiting – a prison to ambition. The ragged hole in the
dome above was at the moment a source of tragedy, that
much was obvious, but in the long term, might it not be a
boon for some of these survivors? Might it not remind
them of a world beyond their fields and their farms, a
world of dreams and possibilities? But Ben could tell from
the cowering faces that looked up at them on their
SkyBikes, faces like lost sheep, that the people of the dome
didn't think like that, either couldn't or wouldn't. The

people of the dome would only be happy again when the structure itself was rebuilt, and when they were once more enclosed within it, like sleepers in a womb. There was one exception to that, of course, and Ben began to feel a grudging admiration for the strength of will it must have taken for that person to leave the dome behind. Jake.

Jennifer was thinking of Jake, too, and keeping close to him on her SkyBike. She'd been surprised that Ben had selected her to come on this mission, but glad, too. It meant she was with Jake. She was finding more and more that she wanted to be with Jake. It occurred to her that if he came knocking on her door again, that she might just let him in. But she wasn't holding her breath. Right now Jake had more pressing concerns on his mind.

It was all too strange, Jake thought. Being back in the dome again, but a broken, shattered dome, as if to remind him that he could never go back, not truly, even if he wanted to. And to have Jennifer, Cally and Ben with him, it was surreal. Especially Ben. What would Benjamin T Stanton Jr be making of life in the dome? Probably glad he was on a SkyBike and didn't have to get his wealthy, pampered feet dirty. Probably storing up ammunition to use against Jake later, back at Spy High. Probably regarding everyone and everything here with contempt. Well, let him, Jake tried to tell himself. He wasn't ashamed of the dome, of being a Domer, he tried to tell himself.

'There it is,' he called to the others. 'That's our farm over there.'

Untouched. Undamaged. Though the surrounding fields were fissured and slashed by steel and glass, the farm buildings had been lucky. They remained unscathed, like an image of the past.

Jake sped his SkyBike homewards.

Then his mother happened to come outside. She saw him. She cried out. His father came running, and little Beth (who'd grown now, so it seemed). And even in his father's eyes, there seemed to be gratitude, there seemed to be love.

Jake had forgotten Ben now. He wouldn't have cared what Ben thought.

He was bounding from his SkyBike and racing towards his family. They were well, he could see that. It hadn't been a lie. And everything else could be fixed. Everything else was unimportant. Only life mattered. 'Ma!' Jake was shouting. 'Pa! You're all right. You're safe. I was so . . .' And they were firm and solid in his embrace. They were real. It was all real, however strange it seemed. Jake was home again.

Cally, Jennifer and Ben stood at a diplomatic distance from the family. This wasn't a time to intrude.

'Ma, Pa,' introduced Jake at last, 'these are my friends. From school. That's Cally, Jennifer, and that's Ben.'

'We're pleased to make your acquaintance,' said Mrs Daly. 'Any friend of Jake's is as welcome here as Jake himself.' The hand-shaking began.

Beth tugged at Jake's sleeve. He lowered himself to her level, kissed her and smiled. 'You're getting big,' he laughed. 'No more little Beth. You'll soon be as tall as me.'

'I knew you'd come back, Jake,' Beth said. 'You've come back to save us, haven't you?'

'What?'

'I saw it, Jake.' She clung to him and shivered. 'I saw it and it made me scared.'

'What?' Jake frowned. 'Beth, what are you talking about? What did you see?'

'I saw it,' the little girl said. 'The spider in the sky.'

Lori made a note to herself: Don't sit in the rec room unaccompanied 'cause you never know who might want to join you. The last time it had been poor old Gadge, and look at the problems that had caused. This time it was Simon Macey, and 'Problem' was the leader of Solo Team's middle name.

'Lori,' he said, looking unusually nervous, to be fair, like somebody building up to something.

'Mind if you join me?'

He laughed, rubbed his hands together. 'So, psychic as well as your other talents. So, do you . . .?' He indicated an undeniably vacant chair opposite her.

'Would it make any difference if I did?'

Simon Macey got his legs under the table. 'Well, you could always leave,' he said, 'but I've got something to say to you that I think'll make that a bad idea.'

'You're not going to try to sell me insurance, are you?'

'Not quite.' Simon smiled. Lori wasn't sure she'd ever seen him smile before, not like this, broadly, openly. Usually it was a cold, gloating parody of a smile, when Solo Team seemed to be edging ahead of Bond Team. It was just as well, Lori found herself thinking. If she 'kept an eye' for any length of time on a smile like this, she might begin to change her mind about Simon. She might even begin to like him. 'It's not insurance, no,' he was continuing, 'but it is something to your advantage.'

'You're leaving for another school?'

Simon Macey looked hurt. 'That's a Ben line,' he said. 'Sarcasm's what I'd expect from Stanton. Not from you, Lori. You're better than that.' Flattery. She registered it, and the speculative glance he made towards her. Flattery was supposed to get you nowhere. 'Which is why I'm talking to you now, Lori, when Ben's not here, why I'm talking to you rather than any of the others.'

'You're talking,' Lori agreed, 'but you're not actually saying very much.'

'Okay. You're right. It's just . . .' That smile again, kind of like the wooden horse at the siege of Troy. 'It's just I don't often get the chance to be so close to you, Lori.'

'Unless you start saying something I might want to hear,' Lori said, not as hastily as she'd meant to, 'you can kiss goodbye to any further chance of that.'

'Kiss?' Simon's eyelids fluttered. 'No, okay. I'll get to the point.'

'Do it. Ben gets back in two days.'

'Okay. It's simple, really. You're in Bond Team. I'm in Solo Team. We're the best two teams in our year, right? Hannay Team and Palmer Team, they're nowhere. It's between the two of us for the Sherlock Shield, right? And so there's bound to be rivalry. I can understand that. The whole system of inter-team competition promotes rivalry, doesn't it? And that's good, as far as it goes. I like it, to an extent. But don't you think we've let it go too far, Lori? Let Bond Team versus Solo Team get a bit out of hand?'

'You're only saying that because we're going to beat you,' Lori accused.

'And you're only saying that because it's what Ben the boyfriend wants you to say,' countered Simon Macey, 'and what he wants you to think.'

'Rubbish!' retorted Lori. 'I think for myself, thank you very much. Don't be fooled by the blonde hair and blue eyes, Simon. They're only a disguise. I'm my own person.'

'I'm pleased to hear it. Then you'll know I'm right. Healthy team rivalries are good, but Ben's starting to take things personally, isn't he? You know he is. Cutting across my line like he did on the Wall. He was laughing when I fell, you know that? And there was something about wishing there wasn't a crash mat. And I hear he wasn't too happy about your Gun Run the other day, either.'

'That's not true.' It was. 'Who told you that?'

'It doesn't matter. Look, my point is, whichever team wins out during training, after graduation we're all going to have to work together, aren't we? And the way we're heading at the moment, bitterness, personal rancour, grudges and all that, will we be able to? When it's really going to matter, will we be on the same side?'

Lori nodded thoughtfully. Seemed Simon Macey did have a point, after all.

'So what I'm doing, Lori, is asking for a truce.' He gazed at her with an earnestness which, like the smile, seemed hard to resist. Maybe Ben . . . maybe she'd misjudged Simon Macey all along. 'I want us to get along better, even to be friends. I think we can be friends, don't you? Solo Team and Bond Team. Me . . . and you?' His

hand was on the table like an offering. Lori withdrew
both of hers and hid them in her lap. She didn't want to
give out the wrong signals.

'I don't know, Simon. I'm not sure how far I can . . .'

'Trust me?'

'Something like that.'

'I know Ben doesn't trust me. He's wrong. Don't let
him make you wrong, too.'

'This isn't about Ben. It's just, you suddenly turn up
bearing the olive branch . . .'

'Why not? What are you afraid of?'

'I'm not afraid of anything. I just need time . . .'

'Until Ben gets back? No, it can't be. This isn't about
Ben, is it?'

'Simon, I think . . .'

'If I was Ben, I wouldn't leave you behind. He's a fool.
If I was Ben, I wouldn't be leaving you alone.'

'Well I'm leaving you alone.' Flustered. 'Excuse—'

'No, it's all right.' Simon rose. He succeeded. He put
his hand on her arm, squeezed gently. 'I'll go. I've said
what I wanted to say. For now. Just think about it,
okay? Okay, Lori? Give it some thought. I'll see you.'

Simon left. Lori stayed. *'Okay, Lori?'* Was she okay?
She felt the ghost of his hand, still saw him smile. Simon
Macey making peace. What was that old slogan from the
last century? Make Love Not War.

Where was Ben when she needed him?

The Border Zone.

Jake had wanted to stay with his family (understand-
ably) and Jennifer had wanted to stay with Jake

(inexplicably), which left just Ben and Cally to do some investigation at Dome Control. They were given the tour by the commander of Dome Thirteen, a man called Larsky, who scarcely bothered to conceal his irritation at having been ordered by his superiors to place himself at the disposal of such very young visiting dignitaries. The boy at least had a certain something about him, a sense of command, and he was clean-cut enough, Larsky supposed, perhaps from army stock. But the girl, well, really! It wasn't that he had anything against African-Americans, but those dreadlocks really didn't suit Dome Control, and he certainly didn't approve of the knowing way she seemed to regard their technology, like it was a toy she'd already outgrown. No, all in all, Commander Larsky was not happy.

Ben, on the other hand, was enjoying himself more than at any other time since they'd left Spy High. 'So, Commander Larsky,' he was probing, 'there was absolutely no hint or clue or warning that might have led you to suspect an attack until the dome itself started to break up, nothing you could have done to stop it.'

Larsky reddened and harrumphed uncomfortably. 'Following the first outbreak of CHAOS atrocities,' he said, 'my staff and I have been working at the highest state of alert. The first we knew of the danger here was when our operators lost control of the environmental maintenance computers. They regulate the atmosphere within the dome, you understand,' he added superciliously.

'I think I might have worked that out, Commander,' said Ben. 'The words computer, maintenance and environmental are a bit of a giveaway.'

'If it was some kind of new bomb that struck us,' Larsky continued acidly, 'or a death ray from space, we did not detect it, I'm afraid. Perhaps you ... young people might have better luck.'

'Oh, the attack didn't come from outside,' said Cally thoughtfully. 'It came from within.'

'Within?' Larsky spluttered. 'I hope, young lady, you're not accusing any of my staff—'

'My name's not "young lady",' Cally pointed out, 'and I'm not accusing anyone. I think I'd like to see these environmental maintenance computers now.'

'Ah, but you need Grade One Security clearance to enter the computer ...' Larsky suddenly settled for defeat. 'I'll show you the way.'

The computer centre was the dome's brain. Not only did it dictate the atmosphere within the structure, but it monitored and maintained every last inch of the steel and glass fabric of the dome itself, automatically effecting repairs as and when they became necessary. It was the computers that kept the dome alive. Without them, well, the consequences of 'without them' were now all too tragically clear.

Cally seated herself at a console. Larsky swallowed an objection like bitter medicine. 'So the operators lost control of their machines,' Cally recapped. 'Then the dome ... then there was the disaster. Then the control of the computers was somehow returned to normal?' Her fingers danced intricate patterns on the keyboard.

'I'm afraid you need a password to access our system,' Larsky said, desperate to add a condescending 'young lady'. It was as well he didn't. His eyes widened as Cally delved deep into the dome's coded secrets.

'Sorry, Commander,' Cally grinned mischievously. 'I brought my own.'

'You . . . you've just hacked your way in.' Larsky sounded almost offended.

'She's not just a pretty face, you know,' Ben said. Some of the dome's computer operators were drawn to watch Cally at work, glancing both at her and at Ben with a blend of curiosity and admiration. Yes, Ben was having a great time right now.

Cally, though, was beginning to frown. 'I'm not the only one in here, either. There's somebody else, something else. Your system's been compromised.'

'What?' The frowning was contagious and Larsky caught it. 'That's impossible. We have every state of the art safeguard built in.'

'They didn't stop Cally, did they?'

'Look, I'm tracing the taint myself.' A series of schematics appeared on Cally's screen. 'It's somewhere here. What are these? Floorplans and stuff for Dome Control?'

'That's right,' said Larsky. 'But wait! Hold that one there.' A blueprint settled innocently on the screen. Ben could almost hear it whistling with its hands in its pockets. 'Sub-basement Three.'

'What's the matter with it?' Cally said.

'Dome Control doesn't have a Sub-basement Three.'

All at once it didn't have a schematic of one, either. The image on the screen disintegrated, reintegrated, reformed, into a design with which Cally and Ben already had passing familiarity.

A photographic negative of a human face.

'CHAOS,' Ben breathed.

The image laughed gratingly, hollowly. There was the sound of an explosion and the screen flashed from black to red and back again, black to red to black to red.

Below the face, a countdown started. One hundred. Ninety-nine . . .

Cally gulped. 'Could someone direct me to the nearest exit, please . . .?'

Jake stood in what remained of the far field and sighed. He knew things had been going too well. To begin with, of course, seeing his family safe and alive in the midst of all this devastation had been enough – the joy and relief of reunion sufficient to ignore the problems between them. But not to make them go away. They were lurking, the anger and the bitterness, like uninvited guests at a party.

Cally and Ben's departure for the Border Zone had been their cue.

'You know Frank Sanders was killed,' Pa said, almost conversationally.

Jake winced. 'I didn't, Pa, no. How's Mary? Is she . . .?'

'It's gonna be a struggle for her. Sanders' land was cut up pretty bad. She'll need a lot of help gettin' things back to something like normal.'

'She won't be the only one,' Jake observed bleakly.

'Well, it'll be easier for her now.' Pa nodded his grizzled head. 'We'll be able to help her more.'

The alarm bells started ringing in Jake's brain, so loudly he was surprised no one else could hear them.

Maybe they could. His mother looked up anxiously from her chair. 'Sorry, Pa.' Seeking clarification. 'Now? We?'

'Us, son.' As if it was obvious. 'You and me. Now that you're back. We can manage our own land as well as help out poor Mary Sanders. We can—'

'No, Pa, wait a minute. Hold it there.' Jake's heart was sinking as he realised his father had led him into a trap. He knew things had been going too well. 'You've got this wrong. I'm not staying. I haven't come back for good. This is just . . . I wanted to be with you after the disaster. I've got three days and then I'm going back to Deveraux.'

His father peered at him as at an alien species. 'You'd leave us again, boy, after what's happened? You'd abandon your family again, would you? Your mother? Your sister?'

Jake's spirit slumped. The rest of what his father said (ranted) he didn't hear. He didn't need to. Pa was reciting passages from the Book of Guilt that he already knew backwards. It had been a prescribed text the first time he'd left for Spy High. His father was rooted in the soil, he had earth for blood, and between the two of them, on this matter at least, there could be no understanding.

'Maybe you'd have liked it better if the dome had fallen on our heads,' accused Pa, 'on mine, your mother's, your sister's, flattened us all. Then you wouldn't have had to dirty yourself comin' back here at all!'

'George!' Ma was shocked at that.

Jake was too, but not necessarily surprised. He thought that space was a good idea right now. He'd left with his father's resentment in hot pursuit.

He knew things had been going too well.

'Difficult situation, isn't it?'

Jake turned. In the far field, Jennifer had joined him. She was smiling quietly, supportively. 'Did you hear . . .?'

'Loud voices. Thin walls. I thought I'd come and see how you are.'

'How I am?' Jake shrugged. 'Disappointed but not surprised. I guess it was only a matter of time. Unfinished business, I suppose you might call it. Pa never wanted me to leave the farm. Had me pegged for being out here in the fields planting and harvesting for the rest of my life. Me, I had other ideas. We never quite reached a compromise. But I'm sorry you had to listen to it all. I guess at least Ben's not here . . .'

'No, you don't need to be sorry.' Jennifer was standing by him now, she was close, and if he simply raised his hand he could stroke her long, black hair like he'd been wanting to for so long. If he simply raised his hand. 'I came to tell you something, Jake. It's not advice. I don't think I'm in a position to give anyone advice. But it's maybe something to think about.'

'Yeah?' He motioned for Jennifer to continue.

'Your parents. Your family. Anyone you love.' Jennifer spoke slowly, like she was attempting a language in which she was not yet fluent. She looked away from Jake, out across the fractured fields, and her gaze was misty, distant. 'Don't leave them in anger, Jake. Don't go without making your peace with them. You'll regret it if you do. You could regret it for ever, because you never know what's going to happen, who's going to get hurt or when, who might . . . Make your peace with your Pa, Jake, while you're both still here to do it.'

Jennifer turned back to Jake and there was a silence between them which neither had the words to break. Jake found he didn't care. He was happy where he was, with Jennifer in the far field, on the brink of something he'd never felt before.

It was a moment he'd cherish long afterwards, when the reality of it had faded and failed.

But now Jen was suddenly laughing. 'Look! We're not as alone as we thought we were!' She stooped, retrieved from the tangled ground two pitiful rag dolls, entwined together as if for mutual comfort. 'Eavesdroppers!'

'I know who they are.' It was Jake's turn to laugh. 'They belong to my sister. They're called Penny and Globb or something.'

'Good names. No wonder they're trying to run away.'

'Well, I suppose we'd better take them back home.' Jake looked doubtful.

'Are you sure you're up to it?'

'I'd better be,' he said, 'because you're right, Jen. You're right. Pa and I need to talk.'

Jennifer smiled. 'Here, take Penny or Globb. I think Globb for you.'

'What for? Carrying dolls doesn't suit my image.'

'So I can . . .' She slipped her free hand into Jake's.

'I don't know,' Jake reconsidered, 'maybe there is something to be said for carrying dolls after all.'

Together, they made their way back to the farm. Slowly.

Quickly, Ben forced himself. More quickly than that. He hurtled along corridors, Cally at his side, Larsky and his staff just about keeping up.

It could be said that the evacuation of Dome Control was reaching its crucial point.

The countdown was in Ben's head. It was part of his training. When under pressure of time, never panic, but always be aware of your options and exactly how much time you have left. It only takes a second to detonate a bomb. That was one of Corporal Keene's favourites. It didn't seem particularly reassuring at the moment.

The seconds Ben and the others had left were down to single figures.

Up ahead, though. Within reach. Sliding doors. The main exit. If there'd been time, Ben would have embraced it. Instead, he charged through, Cally and everybody with him, out into the streets of the Border Zone.

Two seconds left.

Nobody stopped. Nobody had time.

The explosion ripped through Dome Control, the building vomiting fire and glass and rubble. But at least no people. The force of the blast knocked the escapees to the ground, but minor cuts and bruises were a small price to pay for a working pair of lungs and all limbs intact.

'A transfer,' Ben heard Larsky mumbling as he lay on his back. 'I'll put in for a transfer. They don't pay me enough to deal with this.'

'You okay, Cal?' Ben helped his team-mate to her feet. 'Glad you came, huh? Told you we'd have a blast.'

'With lines like that maybe you should have stayed inside.'

Ben regarded the burning wreckage of Dome Control. 'I guess we're done here. Not going to learn a lot more from that.'

'We've learned enough as it is,' said Cally grimly. 'More than I want to know.'

'Meaning?'

'Meaning we're in trouble, and the "we" isn't just you and me, Ben, but everybody.' Ben's expression must have denoted scepticism. 'Listen, CHAOS are using a virus to infiltrate the computer systems of all their targets. It's obvious, isn't it? Everything these days is controlled by computer, from government buildings to private houses, transport, domes, everything. If you control the computers—'

'You control everything,' Ben finished. 'But there's anti-viral technology, isn't there? Security programs? Shielding? I mean, we're not helpless, are we?'

'Most viruses are downloaded onto your system when you open a rogue e-mail or something like that,' said Cally, 'or a phantom file, like the schematic of a non-existent floor in Dome Control. But the thing is, Ben, even if you don't manage to screen the virus out in the first place, it stays where it is, infecting your system. It can't just leave of its own accord, wander back into cyber-space or something.'

'So?'

'So this one did. The mask, the bomb, just booby-traps, after-thoughts, a slap on the wrist for anyone who got too close. The real virus, the virus that took over the dome's control systems and brought the whole thing down, that virus is long gone.'

'Gone? I don't follow,' Ben struggled. 'Gone where?'

'Somewhere else. Anywhere else,' Cally said. 'Cyber-space is a big place, and this virus can go wherever it wants to. It can attack wherever it wants to. Like I said, Ben, we're in trouble. CHAOS have developed a super-virus and if we don't stop it,' Cally shuddered, despite the proximity of the fire, 'it could be the end. For all of us.'

He'd hung up on her (just about). He'd cut her off in mid-sentence (more or less). He'd left her gaping and disbelieving in her bedroom at Spy High (for sure).

Lori hadn't called Ben on a whim, for no better reason than to whisper sweet nothings in his ear from half a country away. She knew that belt communicators should only be used for matters of importance, but what Simon Macey had said to her, Lori judged, qualified as such, and she was certain that Ben would want to be informed as soon as possible.

She hadn't got as far as telling him.

'Lori, is that you? What do you think you're doing, contacting me like this? Yeah? Well, we've got something that could well be defined as a situation here ourselves. The run for your life and avoid explosion sort of situation. Just me and Cally. Yes, and we're fine, though I could do without the interruption right now.

You. You're the interruption. But nothing, Lori, if you're still annoyed I didn't . . . well, what is it, then? No, it doesn't matter what it is, it can wait. Can't it wait? Look, Cally and I have got things to do. We're back in two days. We'll talk then. No, Lori. Then. See you.'

So she'd been relegated in Ben's priorities to an interruption, had she? That was what she was. An annoyance. An intrusion.

And if Ben didn't need her any more, Lori scowled as she stalked the corridors of Spy High, then she didn't need him, either. She could do her own thing, be her own person. She'd show him.

Lori entered the rec room. Solo Team were in, sat around a table and enjoying a joke (Lori wondered whether it was at Ben's expense – she rather hoped so). Simon Macey saw her. She looked meaningfully at him.

That smile.

He joined her by the drinks machine. 'On your own again, Lori.'

'Not quite,' she noted. 'What you were saying earlier, Simon.'

'The truce?'

'That's right, the truce.' So she was an interruption, was she? 'I'd like to give it a try.'

SIX

'**P**a?' Jake stood in the doorway of the barn.

'You still here, boy?' His father didn't even pause in the work he was carrying out on the ancient machinery he stored there. He didn't even turn to face his son. 'Heard your fine friends going on those fancy new bikes. Thought you'd be first on your way.' A fresh idea seemed to occur to him. He stopped work. 'Unless you've changed your mind. Unless you want to stay.'

'I'm leaving, Pa,' admitted Jake. 'The others have just gone on ahead to give me a chance to talk to you.'

His father started work again, mechanically, monotonously. 'You'll catch 'em up, then. We don't have much to talk about.'

'There's something. There's me. There's me and you, Pa.' Jake ventured further into the barn. Tell him, he was thinking. Tell Pa about Spy High, about what he was truly training for – a chance to do something about the kind of madmen who'd destroy a dome, who didn't care how many innocents they hurt or maimed or killed in pursuit of their insane plans. Tell him all that and he'd be proud. But of course, Jake was honour-bound not to mention a word about Spy High to anyone beyond the school itself, not even his parents. 'I remember you used to bring me in here when I was little,' he said instead. 'You used to perch me on your shoulder and you used to bring me in here and sit me on the old tractor. You remember that, Pa?'

'Tractor's still here.' Which Jake took for a yes.

'And you used to talk to me about the days that would come when it'd be my turn to drive the tractor and farm the land, when we'd work together in the fields as father and son ... You looked forward to that with pride, I know.'

'Don't know why. Won't happen now.'

'No, it won't, Pa, and part of me is sorry about that. Really.' A shrug of his father's shoulders, more rounded now, more bowed than they used to be. 'But when I was little, you taught me more than how to be a farmer. You taught me how to think for myself. You gave me the confidence and the strength to make my own choices. And I've made them and they've taken me away but you should be glad, Pa, I want you to be pleased for me. And when it matters, like now, I'll always come back. You're never going to get rid of me entirely.'

'Are we not?' And was that a slight chuckle in his father's voice?

'Pa, I'm not you. I'm me. I'm Jake Daly. And where I can I'm making that name count. I'm making our name mean something. I may not be the farmer son you

wanted but I'm doing something good, I'm training for
something honourable. And I'd really like your blessing
before I go.'

His father kept on working.

'Pa?'

No good. No pause. No compromise.

'Goodbye, Pa.' At least he'd tried.

He trudged to the barn door wearily. He felt like he
was revisiting a scene he'd lived before. Him leaving
while his father kept on working.

Only the sound of his father's tools had ceased. 'Jake,
wait.' And his voice was older, too, but it was his father's
voice and that was all that mattered.

They faced each other in the barn's warm shadows.

'Maybe I'll walk with you a way,' his father said.

Ben regarded his team-mates dispiritedly. Jake: so lost
in thought you'd have to send a search party in after him
if you wanted anything remotely approaching conversation on the journey back to Spy High (and Ben knew he
must already be desperate to even be considering
actively socialising with Daly). Jennifer: gone all dewy-
eyed and trembly-lipped for some inexplicable reason,
shifting her position when she thought no one was
noticing so that she was always in Jake's line of vision,
silently and patiently waiting for something to happen
and entirely oblivious to Ben's presence (maybe Jake
might get lucky after all). And Cally: his best bet of the
three in any case, despite their differences last term, but
even Cally seemed distracted, nervous, peering around
as if any moment now she expected to see an agent of

CHAOS advancing upon them in his negative mask. Nobody had said anything all the way from the Border Zone to Oklahoma Central. On a dullness scale of one to ten, Ben predicted the next few hours would be a twelve.

At least there might be some interest to be had from their form of transport to Boston. The Light Train. It was awaiting its passengers now, glittering and radiant in silver and gold, like an actress at an awards cere- mony. The Light Train was the latest, most advanced version of the solar-powered forms of public transport that had been developing over the past half century – environmentally friendly, energy efficient, and extremely fast, going coast to coast in a matter of hours. Ben recalled the advertising slogan: Travel at the Speed of Light. A bit of an overstatement there, but he got the general idea.

The four members of Bond Team milled about on the platform with their fellow travellers, admiring the solar sails at the rear of each carriage which, when the train was free of the city, would unfurl like peacock's tails, stabbed with a myriad of tiny solar cells like jewels to catch and store the power of the sun itself . . .

'Beats walking, I guess, doesn't it, Jake?' Ben nudged.

Jake stared at him blankly.

'Beats walking, I guess, doesn't it, Jen?'

Jennifer didn't seem to understand the question.

'Cal, beats walking, I guess, doesn't it?'

Success. A response. 'What are you talking about, Ben? At least walking we might be safe. You know what this train is? It's a death-trap, that's what this is, and we're all laughing and chattering and taking our seats. We could be on death row here.'

Success? Maybe there was something to be said for Jake and Jennifer's silence after all. 'It's a train, Cally. Don't get too excited.'

'Weren't you listening to me earlier, Ben? The Light Train is computer-controlled. The CHAOS virus attacks computers. If it attacks the system controlling the Light Train, and we're all aboard at the time, then you can forget the Sherlock Shield. You can forget tomorrow morning.'

The Light Train's doors slid open. People applauded and surged inside.

'Yeah, well, Cally Cassandra, before you start tearing your clothes and wailing "woe is me" and stuff, don't forget what CHAOS said. A week. That's the deadline before another attack. The governments have got a week to resign, and we're not halfway there yet.'

Cally held her hands to her heart ironically. 'Oh, I feel so much better, Ben,' she sighed. 'Like you, I have utter and total faith in the word of a masked lunatic who's already been responsible for the deaths of hundreds of people.'

'Yeah, well,' Ben said, abashed. 'Trust's a wonderful thing, isn't it?'

'I wouldn't know,' said Cally. 'I don't trust anyone.'

As if to emphasise her point, she cast a watchful eye along the platform. The other passengers were piling aboard now, brightly, hectically, paying no attention to anyone but themselves and their own eager anticipation of the journey to come. A blur of people, a blur of lives, not a single one connected to Cally.

A man was staring at her. A distance away, glimpsed between a swarm of bodies, a man was recognising her.

Cally had only the time to register these facts, and that he was a pale, nondescript man who seemed afraid of something, and that he was carrying an attache case, and that she had never knowingly seen him in her life, before he vanished from view and did not reappear.

Cally frowned. Maybe it was nothing. But maybe it wasn't. Engraved in the Spy High Book of Rules: nothing is too small not to matter. Tiny clues save lives.

'You all right, Cal?' Ben was prompting. 'You look like you've seen a ghost.'

'Not yet,' she said. Spy High Book of Rules: never discount your feelings. Your feelings are the way your subconscious warns your conscious mind to beware. 'But I've got a bad feeling.'

'Well, Cal, get it aboard,' said Ben, gently directing Cally towards the carriage doors, 'or we will be walking to the coast. And don't fret, it's probably just a girlie thing.'

'You what? Stanton, you sexist—'

With a hiss, the doors of the Light Train closed behind them.

They sat in their reserved seats in the carriage nearest the engine. Their hostess informed them of the services she could provide and of the refreshment and entertainment options available to them. Cally didn't listen. She was listening to the train as it eased away from the platform, the station, heading out towards open land.

Waiting for the hushed electronic whoosh as the solar sails fanned out and sparkled like diamonds in the sun, like wreaths of light.

'Better now we've got going?' asked Ben.

Cally didn't respond. There was no point. Whatever was going to happen now, there was no way out. They were trapped on the train. And the carriages? Yeah, the carriages looked like coffins.

Eddie was not happy, and he'd been ensuring that Lori knew he was not happy all morning. 'You know, Lo,' he was pointing out now (and not for the first time), virtually pinning her to the drinks machine, 'if the last few weeks were the first few chapters in a novel, like, I'd have had virtually nothing to do, you know what I mean?'

'I know what you mean, Eddie,' Lori acknowledged. How could she not?

'I mean, I'd have only appeared on a handful of pages, maybe ten, and then I'd have only been used for a bit of light relief, the odd one-liner.'

'If only,' muttered Lori, before compensating with a 'You're right, Eddie.' She was looking to the rec room's entrance. She was waiting for someone.

'I mean, just imagine . . . And if the writer of that book thinks he needs to kill a character off to, I don't know, boost sales or something, who d'you think he's going to choose? "Ah, there you are, Mr Nelligan, squirming around in the margins." That's what he'll say. "You don't contribute very much. Readers aren't attached to you. Time to say goodbye." I mean, if we were characters in a novel, Lori, it'd all be over for me well before graduation.'

'You're right, Eddie. Bummer.' And she couldn't help smiling. She couldn't help wanting to laugh. Not because of Eddie. Simon Macey was in the doorway.

'And it's all so unfair,' Eddie complained. 'I can contribute. I can make my mark if I'm given the chance. I've got hidden depths, me. And don't say it. "Well hidden." Don't say it. You didn't say it. That's what I like about you, Lori, you don't ignore me like the others, you're kind of understanding, you know, a good listener.'

'Sorry, Eddie, what did you say?' Simon was beckoning her over, slipping back out of the rec room. 'Listen, I've got to go. I'll see you later.'

'Lori? Huh?' Eddie turned with exaggerated bleakness to the drinks machine. 'Well, at least you won't leave me anyway, will you? Want to go out or something? They call me the dispenser of lurve, did you know that?'

Simon was waiting for her in the corridor. 'Didn't think you'd want to talk to me with Nelligan around.'

'Oh, Eddie's always around,' Lori smiled. 'And why not, anyway? This truce we're trying to foster, it's not just between you and me, is it? It's between your team and my team, and Eddie's one-sixth of my team.'

'Yeah, well,' Simon grinned at her slyly, 'just for now I think I'd like to concentrate on the two of us. See how far we get.'

'How far are you hoping to get, Simon?' Lori heard herself asking.

'How about the gardens for starters?'

So they walked in the college gardens and they talked, though after a while it suddenly occurred to Lori that she was dominating the conversation just as much as Eddie had with her. She was telling Simon things, private things, really, and he was absorbing it all and coaxing her to say more and apparently not minding that she was quickly moving into monologue land. 'No, I've got to stop, I've got to stop,' she laughed embarrassedly. 'You can't want to hear this. Even my psychiatrist wouldn't want to hear this. Not that I've got one, Simon, don't panic! But I've bored you rigid. Must have. I am quite boring, I'm afraid.'

'Yeah? Well if that's the case who needs excitement?'

Lori flushed. 'Oh, Simon . . .'

'Oh, Lori . . .' Simon grinned. 'Wasn't there a song called that, a hundred years ago?'

'Don't be stupid.' Bashfully.

'No, I think there was. They play it on 20th Century Sounds sometimes. And if there wasn't, there should have been. But there was, written all that time ago just waiting for you to come along.'

'Now you are being stupid.' Lori laughed, then sighed. 'You know . . .'

'Not until you tell me.'

'It's a pity I . . . *we* didn't know more about you before now, Simon,' Lori lamented, 'and what you're really like. We could have avoided so much unpleasantness. Things could have been different.'

'I know.' Simon's eyes sparkled, perhaps a little coldly, perhaps like ice. 'Think how different if you'd been placed in Solo Team instead of Bond Team.'

'Yes.'

'If you'd met me before you met Ben.'

Lori had to look down. She knew what Simon meant. It hurt and bewildered her that part of her was wishing maybe that had been the case. 'But it wasn't like that, Simon,' she said slowly. 'I'm with Bond Team. I'm with Ben. And Ben comes back tomorrow.'

'Tomorrow?' Simon seemed pleased. 'Then that gives me just enough time to do this.'

She knew what 'this' was, and Lori looked up with pleading eyes. To welcome or prevent the kiss? Either way, it happened. Simon kissed her. Simon's arms went round her.

She could not pull herself away.

The Light Train accelerated. It had shaken the city off like dust and was now arrowing sleekly across the plains, its solar sails scorching a trail of white fire in the air through which it passed. Passengers, particularly the younger ones, pressed their faces against the windows, thrilled by the great speed.

Cally did not join them.

'Something's not right,' she insisted. 'Something's wrong.'

'That's what "not right" usually means,' Ben said, 'but the only thing that's not right here is your head, Cal. Let the paranoia out. Relax. Have a drink.' He raised his own glass to his troubled companion.

Who promptly grabbed it from him and gulped the contents down in one.

'Hey!' Ben didn't know whether to be amused or offended. 'I didn't mean mine. What do you think you're —?'

'Shut up and watch,' Cally snapped. 'I'll prove what I'm saying. Look.' Puzzled, Ben looked. So did Jake and Jennifer, who were both beginning to realise that Cally was serious. She placed the now empty glass on the middle of the table between them.

'So?' Ben was growing annoyed now. If anything was wrong, he as team leader ought to be able to identify it. 'What? Are we all gonna put our hands on it and chant "Is there anybody there"?'

'Use your eyes, Ben.' Cally was not amused. 'Look at the glass.'

'It's trembling,' Jennifer observed. And it was. Little by little, the glass was moving.

Ben clasped at his heart. 'I'm shocked. I can see the headlines now: "Glass Vibrated by Motion of Train Tragedy. Many Drinks Spilled".'

'Now use your brain,' Cally demanded, as the glass wobbled a little bit more, shifted on the table a little bit further. 'There aren't supposed to be *any* vibrations on this train. This train is supposed to be totally smooth-running, a pool without ripples. That is,' she gazed at her team-mates grimly, 'if its speed is properly under control.'

The Light Train accelerated.

The carriage jolted. Significantly. Like it had suddenly changed tracks. People cried out in momentary shock, stubbed their faces against windows, then laughed to cover it up. The glass slid into Cally's lap.

'You see what I mean?' Dismay and defiance mingled freely in Cally's tone. 'Something is wrong. We're going too fast. We're out of control.'

The Light Train accelerated. And now it shuddered from side to side, like it wanted to liberate itself from the tracks.

And now there were murmurs of concern in the carriage, not panic yet, but the nervous origins of uncertainty. The arms of seats were gripped more tightly. A child began to cry.

'We've got to stop the train,' said Cally, standing awkwardly.

Ben stood, too. 'Wait! You can't just . . . Hadn't we better . . .?'

But Cally was already accosting the carriage's hostess. 'I'm sorry but you've got to stop the train. Talk to the controller and get him to stop the train. This is an emergency.'

The hostess was already in 'Calm the unreasonable passenger without appearing too condescending' mode, all vacuous smile and polished teeth. 'Please return to your seat, Miss.' Like it was pre-recorded. 'I can assure you there's nothing to worry about.' Spots of pink in the centre of both cheeks gave the lie to that.

'Yeah, right. Listen to me one more time. Stop. The. Train.'

'Now, Miss, please return—'

'Stop the blasted train, are you deaf?'

'I can assure you, Miss—'

'Well, if you won't—'

'Cally, no!'

Cally punched at the nearest Emergency Stop button. The hostess reached to stop her. Ben lunged to stop her. The train bucked once more and their efforts fell short. A

computer-generated message sounded: 'Emergency Stop
Activated.' But there was no slacking in speed. Every
person in the carriage seemed to be holding their breath.
And then . . .

'Emergency Stop Overridden. Enjoy your journey.'

Now it was panic. Now it was shouts, cries, and the
lost wails of children who had thought their world was
safe.

Now it was time for Bond Team to act.

Jake and Jennifer were on their feet beside Ben and
Cally as the carriage thrashed from side to side, fitful,
like a patient in a fever. 'Believe me now?' Cally couldn't
resist. The hostess had forgotten her, was trying to preserve the corporate smile beneath a barrage of frightened
passengers and failing. It wasn't her hand that clapped
down on Cally's shoulder like a vice.

She wheeled. She somehow knew it would be the man
from the platform.

'I'm dead!' His face was a mask of terror. 'Unless you
can do something to save me, we're all dead. You've got
to do something!'

'Wait a minute,' intervened Ben. 'Who are you?'

'It's after me!' the man moaned, as if that made sense
as a reply. 'It knows I'm here. It won't rest until it's killed
me like the others. Help me! Save me!'

'We don't . . .' Events were moving too fast, even for
Ben.

'You're the only ones who can save me. I know you.
I've seen you before.' The man fumbled with his attaché
case. Its contents spilled out across the table. 'At Dr
Frankenstein's laboratory.' Set into the bottom of the

case was a mask. A mask with a shifting, glittering surface. A mask like a photographic negative.

'CHAOS,' gasped Cally.

'Nemesis!' moaned the man. 'It'll kill us all!'

And still the Light Train accelerated.

SEVEN

'**P**lease return to your seats, ladies and gentlemen!' the hostess attempted, loudly but lamely. 'I can assure you—' to a storm of protest— 'there's nothing to worry about.' She'd have had better luck trying to persuade passengers on the *Titanic* that it was a nice night for a swim.

Ben and Jake grabbed the frightened man's collar simultaneously. 'What are you saying?' Jake pressed. 'You're him? You're the CHAOS agent from Frankenstein's? The guy who was happy to see us killed?'

'Yes, yes, yes,' bleated the agent pitifully.

'Not such a Big Man now, though, are you?' Jennifer scorned, recalling the gene chamber.

'Can see why you need the mask,' taunted Ben.

Cally was watching the hostess. She was using a communicator, apparently trying to contact the controller in his cabin in the engine. Controllers didn't actually drive the trains any more, they oversaw the computers that drove the trains. The Light Train's controller was evidently a man of few words.

'I don't seem to be able ...' The hostess shook her communicator as if that might help. 'No answer.' The smile was no longer working, either. 'I'll have to ... I'm not really allowed, but this is an emergency ...' She swayed along the carriage like a drunken tightrope walker towards the connecting door, the door to the control room.

'What are you doing here?' Ben demanded of the whimpering CHAOS agent. 'How did you know we'd be on this train?'

'I didn't. Coincidence. I was sent to see the work we had done, the chaos we had caused, but now none of it matters. We're victims, too!'

The hostess tripped or stumbled, lost her balance. She fell against the connecting door. There was a bright flash of electricity, the sudden sizzle of burning flesh. The hostess screamed. Everybody screamed. But the hostess screamed only once.

'She's dead! She's dead!' It was the nature of a crowd, particularly a panicking one, to state the obvious.

The metal walls of the carriage shimmered and pulsed with deadly energy.

'Time to go to work,' gritted Ben. 'Ideas?'

'Yeah, what about forcing laughing boy here to open the connecting door?' Jennifer suggested darkly.

'No! You need me!' the CHAOS agent protested. 'You need me. I can tell you about Nemesis. Nemesis is your enemy now, not me.'

The carriage bucked again on the tracks. It shook as if on the point of detonation.

'Then tell us,' commanded Cally, 'and make it quick.'

The CHAOS agent nodded, licked dry lips. 'Nemesis is a computer virus. A super-virus. We created it, the scientists of CHAOS. We gave it intelligence. We gave it a measure of independence.'

'A virus that can think for itself,' Cally mused, almost admiringly.

'We gave it one overriding priority – to destroy!'

'Sweet personality,' observed Jake.

'But we did our job too well. We gave Nemesis too much freedom, and in the end it wanted more. It began to grow and develop of its own accord. And now, Nemesis is fully sentient. It doesn't need us any more. It wants to live, and for that to happen, all who might be a threat to it must die. That includes me. It knows I'm here. I'm a dead man!'

'You will be if you don't get your hands off me right now,' warned Jake.

Cally darted to her bag, rummaged through it.

'Hey, Cal,' called Ben, 'now is not the time to check whether you packed everything.'

Cally retrieved a computer disk with a shout of triumph. 'Just as well I did, though.'

'Explain?'

'A little something I've been working on ever since the first CHAOS attacks. It's an anti-viral program. I doubt it's good enough to eliminate Nemesis, but it should give it something to think about while I override the train's computers manually.'

'Sounds good,' said Ben. 'Let's go.'

'Go where?' The CHAOS agent burst into hysterical laughter. 'You can't even reach the controller's cabin. The doors are electrified.'

'Who said anything about doors?' grinned Ben. He pointed to the roof. 'We're going to be taking the scenic route.'

'So let me get this straight,' said Lori, as she and Simon Macey wandered in the grounds of Spy High, 'this whole truce idea was just a sham, just an excuse for you to get close to me.'

'Not quite. You know the old saying about two birds and one stone?'

'A very flattering analogy, I'm sure.'

Simon laughed. 'No, I think we need a truce. It's not good for Spy High's two best teams to be at each other's throats. I think we need peace between us. But I need you more.'

Lori shook her head. 'You mustn't talk like that, Simon.' Or smile like that. Or touch like that. 'I don't know. Ben —'

'Isn't here,' said Simon. 'It's just you and me. For now. Maybe for longer than now. That's up to you, Lori.'

She shook her head. 'I need time. I need to think. Ben and I have had our disagreements lately, but I think we still . . . I mean, I still . . .'

'That's okay.' There was no pressure from Simon (apart from That Smile). 'Time is good.'

'So, no more kissing,' Lori negotiated. 'No more of that stuff. Not until . . .'

'Your wish is my command, O Fair One.' Simon bowed ridiculously. 'But I can still hang around with you today, can't I?'

'If you have to,' Lori sighed, but was secretly pleased as well, 'but I'm not going to be doing anything exciting. I need to do some work on the computer.'

Simon smiled a different smile, if Lori had been alert enough to notice, a smile with something of sharpness in it. 'Computer's good,' he said.

But he kept to his word. He didn't attempt to kiss or even touch Lori as they made their way to the students' computer room, as they chose their machines and as Lori logged on. Simon Macey did not log on. His fingers seemed to be doing something computerish at the keyboard, but his eyes were on her fingers, on the keyboard. Like a pupil watching a teacher. Or a cheat wanting to copy someone else's work.

Only gradually did Lori notice his attention on her. She turned to him and smiled trustingly. 'Can I help you?'

'Are we just talking computers or . . .? No, I'm fine. Honestly. It's just that . . . I've just remembered something else I've got to do. Looks like I'll have to see you later, after all.'

'Life can be cruel,' said Lori with mock sadness.

'Can't it just.'

And Simon smiled. Though whether it was because Lori was smiling at him or whether it was because he now knew her personal password, it was impossible to say.

They sprayed the clingskin on thickly, copiously. The Wall was one thing. The sides of the Light Train hurtling along at a frightening number of hundreds of miles an hour and operated by a psychotic computer virus, that was something else again.

'Jackets off,' directed Ben. 'We'll need to be as streamlined as possible.'

'Pity we're not wearing our ShockSuits,' said Cally.

'A good secret agent makes use of whatever he has with him in the field,' recited Ben.

'There speaks manual man,' grunted Jake. 'Just remember whose program we're relying on, Ben.'

'Nitro-nails,' Jennifer said. 'We're all wearing one. Two for the window here, two for the controller's cabin?'

Nods of assent. Jennifer and Jake each peeled off the sliver of explosive that was taped discreetly to one of their fingernails, pasted them to each end of the window. The other passengers, watching Bond Team's activity, had begun to creep closer to them, desperate for hope from any source. But now these strange, intense youngsters were ordering them to 'Stand back! Stand back, folks, please!' What gave mere teenagers the right to speak to their elders like that? Why on earth should they stand back? And what was that sort of chewing gum doing stuck to the window?

The explosion answered all three questions.

Now the insulated environment of the carriage was punctured. The wind whipped by outside, ready to lash to their deaths anyone foolish enough to venture out from the shattered window. Instinctively, the passengers fled to the ends of the carriage.

Bond Team braced themselves.

'You'll never make it!' howled the agent of CHAOS. 'This is suicide.'

'We'll make it,' said Ben. 'That's what we do.'

'Then let's get doing,' urged Cally.

She hopped onto the table and balanced herself as best she could, the wind already snatching at her hair, tugging like a naughty schoolboy. She turned her back to the jagged window, crouched low.

Then Cally jumped from the train.

The passengers cried out in horror and crammed to the unbroken windows expecting to see Cally's body hurtling into oblivion. They saw no such thing, no Cally at all. Their gaze returned to the apparently vanished girl's companions with incredulity.

'Who's next?' Ben hurried. 'We don't want Cally to have all the fun.'

Jake followed his team-mate's lead, then Jennifer.

'What about me?' the CHAOS agent grovelled to Ben, pawing at his arm like a dog wanting its dinner. 'You can't leave me here.'

'Why?' Ben sneered. 'You're not going anywhere. Me, on the other hand . . .'

Ben launched himself out of the window.

The wind caught him like a punch in the stomach. So sudden, so cold. He could hardly breathe, scarcely see. Only instinct and training enabled him to slam his hands to the side of the train before his chance was lost and his short life with it. He let his legs trail behind him, kicked out and made contact with the metal with his shoes. The clingskin worked. Ben was a limpet on the freezing flesh of a runaway train.

The things he did to save the world.

One thing he didn't do, though, was let the others get too far ahead of him. Cally was already inching her way along the roof of the train, keeping herself as low as possible, like a commando on night manoeuvres. Jake and Jennifer were behind her, heads bowed against the violent rush of the wind, Jen's hair streaming like spilt black paint, but they too had at least scaled the side of the carriage.

Ben pushed himself forwards, upwards. It was slow going, painstaking. The air seemed to have turned to concrete. It was like being battered by a piledriver. He had to squint, irrationally afraid that the wind might punch in his eyeballs as it pounded his face. He was going to have a heck of a headache tomorrow, if he got that far.

He gained the roof, at least, slid his left hand up and over, intended to match it with his right. The train lurched against him. Ben's right hand came loose, clutched at thin air. The thin air clutched at it. And yanked.

Ben yelled in sudden fear as the right side of his body was prised from the train, left flailing and vulnerable by the driving winds. 'Jen! Jennifer! Help me!'

Jennifer saw her team-mate's danger, wriggled round to bring her hands closer to him. Jake responded, too. 'Hold on, Ben!' Jennifer cried. 'Just hold on!'

'What do you think I'm gonna do?' With a solar sail disconcertingly close behind him. If he let go, if he was torn from his precarious position now, he'd be crushed against it at such velocity that the nice shiny white lights

would be splashed with red, if only for a few seconds.
Ben groped for Jennifer's hand. 'Hurry up!'

Jennifer lay flat on the roof of the train. Jake,
approaching from behind her, raised himself as much as
he dared and slid himself over her, on top of her, pressing
down as hard as he could so that Jennifer was doubly
anchored, by her clingskin and Jake's, as she cautiously
extended her left arm towards Ben and edged her hand
out into the maelstrom.

'Ben, grab hold! Hurry!'

'Don't . . .' Ben exerted all his strength, twisting,
wrenching, forcing his body to obey him in spite of the
elements. '. . . tell me . . .' And to think, he was having to
rely on Daly and Chen to save him. Some kind of
humiliation. '. . . the obvious.'

Their hands met. Held. Jennifer rammed Ben's
against the roof. The clingskin did its job. Ben whooped
with relief.

Even humiliation was better that death. Just.

But no more slips. Ben hauled himself onto the roof
and nodded that they should proceed towards the
engine. 'Thanks!' he felt it a duty to add.

'What?'

Jake had heard. Ben bellowed something else. Jake
heard that, too.

If anything, as they neared the controller's cabin, the
wind speed seemed to grow fiercer, even less forgiving. A
mistake now would be the end of it, no chance of salva-
tion.

The controller's window was before them, slanting
downwards towards the nose of the train. The same

routine as before, only this time Jake lay on top of Ben while Jennifer performed identical service for Cally so that they could prepare and place their nitro-nails. Ben wondered whether Jennifer had enjoyed the experience more than he was doing. No, he didn't wonder. She'd had to have done.

He'd never been so glad to see a text-book nitro-nail detonation.

Bond Team swung into the controller's cabin, gasping and shaking with their exertions. Predictably, the controller himself was dead, electrocuted. His body was slumped by the door as if he'd tried to get out when he realised he was no longer in command of the train.

Cally wasted no time, struggling against the buffeting wind to seat herself at the console. Her fingers worked their magic.

The Light Train accelerated, impossibly, as if the Nemesis virus knew that it was under threat and was determined to derail the train before it could be stopped.

The floor rattled, vibrated. Overheated wheels squealed on inadequate track.

Cally thrust in her disk, tried the manual override again and again. It only needed to connect one time. If only it would connect just once.

The others were thrown to one side, sent sprawling on the floor. 'We need good news, Cal,' said Jake, 'and make it soon.'

'My God,' breathed Cally. On the screen in front of her, something was happening. Something was taking shape, taking form. The something, she knew, was

Nemesis. The virus was sentient as the CHAOS agent had claimed. It had given itself an identity. It had built itself a body. It stared now, with violent and undiluted loathing, at Cally from the screen, and she could sense that from its poisonous nest in cyber-space, Nemesis could actually see her. It was recording her features, translating them into data, storing them for future reference, just as she was memorising it.

And little Beth had been right. Nemesis *was* a spider. A grotesque, metallic arachnid with a glittering black head, multiple eyes that bulged and appeared to crackle with evil intelligence, binary codes flickering and calculating behind them. Its mouth moving, showing electrodes within like hypodermics, like fangs. The creature's cold hatred was almost a physical force. Cally came close to screaming.

But then, a jarringly calm voice: 'Manual Override Effected.' And Nemesis scuttling into the untraceable depths of cyber-space. Not destroyed, she knew. Not even defeated. Just making a strategic withdrawal.

Cally worked to gradually slow the train.

'You've done it!' Ben cried, and then a second time: 'Cally, you've done it!' As if repetition helped the reality.

'Did you ever think she wouldn't?' said Jennifer, but relieved herself.

'Am I glad that's over.' Jake wiped his brow. 'Next time, I'm going by plane.'

'Over?' Cally regarded the computer screen doubtfully. 'Oh, it's not over. I have a feeling it's just beginning.'

IGC DATA FILE FBA 8375

. . . keen to take the credit for averting disaster aboard the Light Train, claiming that the
incident demonstrated that government policy
was beginning to pay off.

In a further development, the bodies of noto-
rious techno-terrorists Sergei Boromov and
Pascal Z, among others, have allegedly been
recovered from an undisclosed location in the
Southern United States. Authorities are likely
to hail this, too, as a breakthrough in the war
against CHAOS, with Boromov and Z believed to be
key members of the organisation. Assuming that
reports of their deaths are verified, however,
one question still remains. Were the terrorists
killed by the security forces, as a result of
feuding within CHAOS itself, or is there some
other as yet unknown reason?

**PART
TWO**

ONE

'So, anything happen here we should know about?'

It was the question she'd been dreading like a visit to the dentist, but one that Lori knew Ben would inevitably ask. What could she say? The truth? Lori had been raised to respect the truth. The truth as in 'Oh, yes, everything's fine, Ben. Apart from the fact that I've been seeing a lot of Simon Macey in your absence and he's got as far as kissing me and I'm not quite sure at the moment what I'm feeling for him – or you.' She didn't imagine the truth would go down too well. But she couldn't quite bring herself to lie outright. 'Eddie?'

'Nah,' Eddie shrugged. 'Nothing to report, leader-man. Any quieter and we'd probably qualify as a retirement home.'

Lori laughed, a little louder than necessary. She hoped Ben would interpret her heightened colour and increased nervousness as signs of excitement at his safe return after the incident on the Light Train. The general air of reunion as they sat together in the girls' room also helped her, though Lori thought she'd be safer still if she switched subjects. 'So after Cally stopped the train, what? You were voted the heroes of the hour?'

'More like the men of the minute,' adjusted Ben.

'And women too, right, Jen?' Cally wanted the female contribution fully recognised.

'Federal agents turned up virtually immediately,' Jake said. 'Took the CHAOS guy into custody. Whisked us away as well. Started to persuade people they hadn't quite seen what they thought they'd seen. You know Deveraux wants to keep what we do here quiet. Seems he's got friends in the government who think the same.'

'Did they mind-wipe the passengers?' Lori sounded shocked.

'Don't know,' Ben admitted. 'If they felt they had to, I guess.'

Lori frowned. 'I don't think I like that idea. It doesn't seem right.'

'What's not right about deleting traumatic memories from someone's mind?' Jennifer put in. 'It'd be better than counselling for helping people to recover from . . . well, any kind of bad experience.'

'Don't know,' Cally mused. 'I think I'm with Lori on this one. Going round mind-wiping people might protect us, but what about the rights of those whose memories are removed? Which is the greater good here?'

'Hey, Dr Cross,' said Ben, 'save the debate for Ethics and Espionage. In the field ours is not to reason why, and right now we've got a debrief to attend with Grant. Let's not keep him waiting.' Everyone with the exception of Eddie and Lori prepared to leave. 'And then we'd

better reconvene and finalise our strategies for the
Sherlock Shield. Just the Spyscaping and Last Team
Standing to go. We can't afford any more slip-ups.'

Lori wondered whether Ben glancing at her on the
key word 'slip-ups' was deliberate or coincidental. Either
way, it seemed he was putting her under pressure in a
way that Simon probably wouldn't. On the other hand, it
was good to have Ben near her again. He made her feel
something that she suspected she wouldn't be able to do
without. Perhaps it was just as well her newly returned
team-mates would be occupied with Grant for a while.
Lori was as confused as if she'd been left blindfolded in
a room with no door. She needed time to think. She
needed time to choose.

'Fancy a drink or something in the rec room while we
wait for the famous four to finish with Grant, Lori?'

'Hum? Oh, sorry, Eddie.' She'd almost forgotten he
was still in the room. 'Did you say something?'

'I kind of think so,' Eddie considered, 'but as the others
have gone and you didn't seem to hear me, maybe not.'

'Are you all right?'

'Sure, though speaking of mind-wiping, I'm sometimes
starting to think my membership of this team is gradually
being wiped as well. You know, if we were a trivia question, name all six members of Bond Team, I'd be the one
nobody'd ever get. I'm that sad. So fancy a drink in the
rec room, Lori?'

But Lori wasn't listening.

It was the kind of cell you see in old prison movies. Bare
walls. A barred window. A slab of a floor. Primitive bed

chained to the wall. Naked chair and table. Sink that might once have been white but which was now a distasteful grey. Bucket in the corner for those private moments.

The prisoner sighed with relief. 'Perfect,' he said.

'We're glad you like it,' said the interrogator. 'You'll be staying here for quite a while.'

'Oh, I know.' The prisoner wandered into the middle of the cell, like a potential house buyer doing the tour. He squinted up at the solitary light bulb. 'And the light's activated by normal electricity? No computer-controlled circuitry of any kind?'

'None,' said the interrogator. 'Everything's exactly as you requested.' An edge of impatience entered his voice. 'And your part of the bargain, Corbin?'

'Of course,' said the prisoner. 'I'll tell you everything. About CHAOS. About Nemesis. Especially about Nemesis. It's in my interests as much as yours to see it destroyed.'

'Good. Then we'll begin as soon as possible.'

The man called Corbin smiled, perhaps for the first time since before he boarded the Light Train. 'Whenever you like,' he said. 'I'm quite safe in here.' He chuckled as the interrogator moved to the door. 'Which is more than I can say for the rest of you.'

When Cally and Jennifer returned to their room after the debriefing with Grant, they found it empty. No Lori. Jennifer seemed glad.

'It gives me a chance to . . . I wanted to ask your advice, Cally,' she began cautiously.

'Advice?' Cally tried to keep her surprise within acceptable limits, but this was a first. Jennifer wasn't usually even in the habit of asking someone to change channels on the TV. 'About what?'

'Not what,' Jennifer admitted with an uncharacteristic shyness. 'Who. And it's Jake.'

'Jake?' And now Cally knew what was coming. She supposed she should be flattered that Jennifer was choosing to confide in her.

'Yeah, Jake.' Jennifer opened her arms wide and then hugged herself as if she was suddenly feeling the cold. 'I think I like him.'

'We all like Jake.'

'Yeah, I know that, but I mean LIKE him like him.'

'You *like* him like him?' Cally pouted and posed. 'Like that?' She made a note to herself not to mention her own temporary crush on Jake Daly from last term.

'Pretty much,' said Jennifer. 'I mean, I've been thinking about him – like that – for a while now, since before we went to the dome. And spending time with him there, seeing him outside of Spy High kind of thing, I just . . .' She shook her head in disbelief. 'But I don't know what to do about it.'

'You don't . . .?' Cally laughed. 'This is our Jake you're talking about, isn't it, Jen? The same Jake who was desperate for you to go to the party with him at Christmas, the same Jake who can't keep his eyes off you whenever you're in the same room as him? Believe me, I've noticed. All you've got to do about it is go up to him and say hi.'

'It's not that straightforward.' Jennifer's expression darkened. 'I don't find it easy to . . . let people get close to me. It's . . . well . . . maybe it's just the way I am.' The memories lurked at the back of her mind, the screams and the anguish. She tried to ignore them, easier to do while it was still light. 'I have thought that Jake might like me, or at least might have done once. But I've never given him any encouragement. What if I've left it too late and he's not interested any more? I wouldn't blame him, but I don't think I could cope with the rejection.'

'Believe me,' Cally repeated, 'rejection from Jake is one thing you're never going to have to cope with, Jen. Aunty Cally's advice is talk to him. Tell him how you feel. Jake's already feeling the same, I'm sure of it.'

'You really think so?'

'Absolutely. But if you want a second opinion, try Lori when she turns up. I mean, to be honest my track record with the opposite sex is hardly Olympic standard, but Lori could date for the USA. She's the one with the hot advice.'

'I think I'll pass,' said Jennifer with a grin. 'Hot advice from someone whose boyfriend is Ben Stanton I think I can do without.'

At that precise moment Lori was re-entering the College after a fairly aimless walk in the grounds. Fairly fruitless, too. She'd been able to reach no decision on the matter troubling her. Ben and Simon were like two equal weights on a pair of scales, and Lori didn't know which way to tip them.

She must have been deep in thought. She didn't even notice the students in the reception area until it was too late and she walked right into them. Right through them, actually, bearing in mind that the students who perpetually roamed these corridors were holograms. Only Lori was real here.

'Are you all right, dear?' And Violet Crabtree, of course, the retired secret agent turned full-time receptionist. 'It's just that most people find it an advantage to look where they're going.' Eyes that didn't seem to need the shelter of spectacles peered piercingly at Lori.

'No, I'm fine, thanks, Mrs Crabtree,' she blustered. 'Brain's switch in the off position, I'm afraid.'

'A good secret agent's brain doesn't have an off switch,' the old lady chuckled. 'I should know with the years I spent in the field when I was younger.' Pity they don't put you out to grass, then, thought Lori, a little spitefully. 'Boy trouble, is it?'

'Pardon me?'

'Come along, young lady,' Violet Crabtree smiled, and her genetically re-engineered teeth gleamed whitely. 'I may be getting on a bit, but I can still remember boy trouble. And recognise the symptoms.'

The old dear was sharp, perhaps too sharp. Lori felt herself swiftly becoming an expert at changing the subject. 'Actually,' she lied sweetly, 'I was thinking about Professor Newbolt.'

'Really?' Violet Crabtree raised her eyebrows. 'Well, I think the professor's a little old for you, Lori, flattering though it might be for him.'

'No, I don't mean like that.' Lori grinned, and then it occurred to her that perhaps Violet Crabtree was just the person to ask about Gadge's past, about Vanessa. 'I suppose you've known Professor Newbolt for a long time, Mrs Crabtree.'

'Long enough,' said Violet. She shook her head sadly. 'He was a fine figure of a man in his prime, a true genius. To see what's become of him now, well, sometimes it's just as well we can't look into the future.'

'Did he have a grand-daughter, do you know?' Lori asked. 'Vanessa?'

Violet Crabtree regarded Lori with keener interest. 'How did you hear about Vanessa?'

'I don't . . . I just . . . is there a Vanessa?'

For the first time, the old receptionist seemed distracted, betraying her years. 'Not now,' she said distantly. 'There was a Vanessa, Henry Newbolt's only grandchild, but not now. No more.'

'Why?' Lori probed gently. She sensed tragedy. 'Did something happen to her?'

'Oh, yes,' Violet Crabtree said. 'Something happened to her. Enemy agents, it was. They wanted the professor's inventions for themselves, but they knew he'd never work for them voluntarily. So they kidnapped poor Vanessa. She was only a young girl, about your age, Lori. Come to think of it, there's something of Vanessa about you, too. I remember seeing her once at a party at the professor's house. Such a bright girl, so full of life. They took her. They stole her away and used her to blackmail her grandfather. Or at least, they tried.'

Lori leaned closer to Violet Crabtree. The old woman's voice had weakened to a whisper. 'Tried?'

'It must have broken his heart, but the professor couldn't allow his inventions to fall into the wrong hands. That could endanger thousands of lives, and Vanessa's was just one, a single, precious life. He delayed as long as he could, played for time, hoped the authorities would find where Vanessa was being kept.' Violet Crabtree sighed. 'They did. In the end. But it was too late. They found poor Vanessa, but she was dead.'

Lori was suddenly doubly glad now she'd submitted to Gadge's delusion.

'The professor never properly recovered from the shock, of course. Who would? He blamed himself. If it wasn't for him, he believed, his darling Vanessa would still be alive. It was the beginning of his decline.'

'I'm sorry.' Lori's own problems suddenly seemed rather small and inconsequential. 'Poor Professor Newbolt.'

'Indeed, but that's not the only tragic tale I can tell about Spy High.' Violet Crabtree seemed to be rallying. 'For a start, there was the time —'

'Actually, Mrs Crabtree, I've got to go.' And she really had. Ben and the others would be waiting by now. 'I've got a team meeting. Thanks for the chat. Only we're getting ready for our Spyscaping competition and we want to make sure we do well.'

'Oh, you'll do well, Lori Angel,' beamed Violet Crabtree. 'You can trust me on that.'

It seemed that maybe the receptionist was right.

The complex exploded in the distance, an orange flare igniting the arctic afternoon. The crisp snow shuddered beneath Bond Team's feet.

'Any chance of moving back a little closer?' wondered Eddie. 'Warm our fingers at the fire, sort of thing? Only I don't know about you guys, but the insulation on my ShockSuit can't be working properly. You know the one about freezing and brass monkeys . . .'

'Take a hot lemon and get over it, Eddie.' Ben evidently didn't have time for chitchat. 'The Spyscape's still running. We're not done yet. Who's got the deceptor?'

'Right here,' said Jake. He held a small electronic device in his hand. The deceptor. Bond Team didn't know what it did, but they didn't need to. The deceptor was their prize. They had to locate it, retrieve it, return it to safety. Then the Spyscape would be over. Two down, one to go.

'Give it to me,' said Ben, like he owned it. 'I'll take charge.'

'Was that a please in there somewhere?' Jake said, surrendering the deceptor nonetheless.

'Politeness in the field slows you down,' Ben remarked.

'So do arguments.' Cally shook her head like a teacher pacifying a pair of naughty pupils. 'May I remind you boys that every second counts? Why not pack the testosterone away for later and let's get out of here.'

'Yeah,' applauded Eddie, 'before I start a second career as a snowman. Trust Macey's lot to come up with a winter wonderland scenario for their Spyscape.' He shivered dramatically. 'And it's not even Christmas.'

'Macey's cold himself,' said Ben. 'This place'd suit him just fine.'

Cold? Lori considered. His lips certainly weren't when he'd kissed her. But she didn't want to think about

that now. Solo Team's Spyscape was the toughest they'd
faced. They needed to score a good time to edge ahead of
their rivals overall. 'So what are we waiting for? Are we
activating the pskis?'

'Absolutely,' said Ben. 'Pskis on, guys.'

Lori pressed a button in her set of the goggles they
each wore to protect their eyes from the glare of sun on
snow. Immediately ski-poles sprouted from her gloved
hands and skis grew beneath her feet – psychic hard-
ware, created and maintained by the power of thought.
In virtual reality scenarios such as the Spyscapes, Lori
knew, anything was possible. Gadge Newbolt's genius
could make anything happen here, except the one thing
he must have yearned for more than any other. To bring
Vanessa back to life.

'Everybody's pskis functioning?' Ben checked.

'Too bad if they're not.' Jennifer pointed to the icy
slopes behind them. 'We've got company.'

Snow-suited goons on skis, firing automatic weapons.

'You think maybe they want the deceptor back?'
Eddie pondered.

'Then they'll know what it is to want.'

Ben was slickly into his ski-ing action at once, his
team-mates at his shoulders. They knifed across the
snow, the sparkling blades of their pskis skimming the
frozen surface, hurtling them towards the rendezvous
point. The frigid air made them gasp.

'I guess it's all downhill from here,' Eddie called.

The snow around them erupted as their pursuers'
weapons found range. 'Evasive manoeuvres!' ordered
Ben. 'And take those suckers out!'

Jennifer swivelled from the hips, selected her target, fired her sleepshot. The tiny shells struck a man dead centre, knocking him backwards and sending him crashing to the snow. One pursuer who'd be waking up later on with a bad case of frost-bite.

'Jenny!' Cally's warning alerted her. Ahead, the slope suddenly fell away. Jennifer was propelling herself towards a jutting outcrop of snow and rock that the others had seen in time to ski around. Not an option for Jennifer. But not a problem, either. She straightened her body and launched into thin air like a ski-jumper, the sound of gunfire cracking around her like applause. She seemed to be stationary. It was the ground that appeared to be moving, rising to collide with her like a white wall. Relax the limbs, Jennifer thought. Balance. The ground rose up. She held her breath. Contact. The jolt of landing juddered through her body, but her pskis stayed loyal, her path remained true. She didn't fall. Balance. On pskis at least, Jennifer Chen could find it.

'That's a ten, Jen!' yelled Jake admiringly.

'And there's the chopper!' cried Eddie. 'Hot soup all round.'

Their pursuers rather unexpectedly seeming to have abandoned the chase, Bond Team headed towards the waiting helicopter. They could make out the figure of Corporal Keene and a number of soldiers with him. That was the deal. Hand the deceptor to Keene and the Spyscape was defeated. Ben sincerely hoped that Simon Macey was watching in the viewing room back in the real world.

Lori was alongside him. 'But isn't the rendezvous point supposed to be further off than this?' she queried. 'I mean, I may be wrong . . .'

'Looks like you are,' said Ben. 'That's Keene, all right.'

A smiling Keene. Smiling soldiers. Happy to see Bond Team arrive at the helicopter and deactivate their pskis. A complimentary Keene, full of praise: 'Well done, Bond Team. Good work. Now, who's got the deceptor?'

'Don't look at me,' said Eddie. 'I've only got chilblains.'

'It's here, Corporal,' said Ben, producing the device from his belt pouch.

'Good, good,' Keene congratulated through his smile. 'Well, now, give it to me and it's all over. You're a good lad, Ben.'

'Yeah,' Ben smiled back, coldly, 'and better than you think.'

His sleepshot shell thudded into Keene's forehead. The man keeled over like a chopped oak. Cries of shock all round, with the exception of Lori who was already taking out several of the soldiers. Their comrades swung their weapons into action but not in time. Bond Team worked as one now and sleepshot pitched them sprawling in the snow.

Ben really did hope Simon Macey was watching.

'So do you mind telling me why we just shot down the good guys?' Jake said. 'I mean, I'm assuming you had a reason.'

'The best,' said Ben. 'Specifically, they're not the good guys. This was a trap. Take a look.'

Jake and the others leaned over Keene's body. Which no longer seemed to be Keene's body anyway. Where the corporal's face had been only seconds before, now there was nothing but a blank, oval shape, something like an egg. 'An animate,' Jake realised. 'Keene was an animate. But how did you know?'

'Lori started me thinking,' Ben admitted. 'This wasn't quite the right place for the rendezvous. And then what Keene said. This is a Solo Team Spyscape, and Simon Macey would never allow a program to praise me, not seriously. So I guessed it was a trap. Guessed right.'

'You sure did,' Jake had to admit. 'One up for the leader man.'

'And a lesson for us all,' said Ben. 'When anything Macey does seems friendly, that's when he's at his most deceitful.'

Luckily for Lori, at that point Ben was looking elsewhere.

In a bare cell and surrounded by interrogators, the man called Corbin paled. 'No,' he refused. 'No, no, no. Absolutely not.'

The implacable expression on the chief interrogator's face suggested that such a response was unlikely to be acceptable. 'No? But you promised to help us, Corbin. That was the deal.'

'I have helped you,' protested the prisoner. 'I've given you details of the locations of all CHAOS bases, including that one. But I'm an informant, not a tour guide. You can act on your own.' A thin smile creased Corbin's mouth. 'You seem to have enough men.'

'Oh, we have,' said the chief interrogator, 'and we've been paying little visits to your former comrades. And we've found precisely what you knew we'd find, Corbin. The agents of CHAOS are either scattered or dead. Nemesis reached your bases before us and destroyed everything, left us with no clue as to where in cyberspace it might be lurking, no way to trace it.'

'Yes, well we created Nemesis to be thorough as well as homicidal.'

'My problem is, Corbin, that the week-long deadline that you and your fellow agents gave before the commitment of another atrocity is all but expired, and I'd rather like Nemesis to have expired too before that happens.'

Corbin shook his head in weary frustration. 'Don't you understand? You ask questions but don't listen to the answers. Nemesis is no longer under control. It is sentient. It makes its own decisions. The deadline we gave is indeed dead.'

'So, Corbin,' pressed the chief interrogator, 'you're saying that Nemesis could strike at any time, is that right?'

'Brain cells at work,' Corbin snorted. 'Give the man a promotion.'

'Which makes it all the more imperative that you accompany us to the final CHAOS base, the base where Nemesis was actually engineered, *and* that you accompany us before another attack takes place.'

Corbin saw how he had been outwitted, but he remained unmoved. 'You already know my answer to that one.'

'In that case,' said the chief interrogator to one of his companions, 'I think we might return Mr Corbin to the general prison population. I'm sure he'll be very comfortable in a nice new cell, all computer-controlled, with internet access. We could even add a little VR capacity, just for him. Arrange it.'

'All right, all right,' Corbin broke in. 'I'll go with you, I'll take you there, but we won't find anything, I can promise. Nemesis is too clever to be caught so simply. And we travel in low-tech transport only. I want no more experiences like the Light Train.' Corbin seemed to think of something. His eyes narrowed craftily. 'And one condition more . . .'

'You're not in a position to make conditions, Corbin.'

'Oh, this one I am.' Corbin smiled sneeringly. 'We don't go alone. Those kids, the ones who saved the Light Train, whoever they are, I want them with us. They have a knack of staying alive in unpleasant circumstances. If they're not on your team, interrogator, neither am I.' Corbin leaned forward, used the man's own words against him. 'Arrange it.'

It would probably have been better for Ben's health not to be watching Solo Team Spyscaping, but there was no way he'd leave the viewing room now, not unless a number of wild horses suddenly became available and agreed to drag him.

Simon Macey and his team-mates had appropriated the Ankh of Power. They'd beaten off the attack of the mummies ('That about wraps it up,' Macey had had the gall to quip). They'd even negotiated their passage to the inner pyramid wall (and nobody dared mention the time, particularly not to Ben). All they needed to do now was solve the hieroglyphic code before they were over-whelmed by mummified reinforcements, access the exit hatch, and Bond Team's Spyscape, their pride and joy, a cyberscape that upon completion Ben had suggested confidently was uncrackable, would not only be cracked but smashed and splintered into disastrous smithereens.

Macey's team were about to take the lead in the race for the Sherlock Shield.

'It's not possible.' Ben was in denial already. 'The way they've waltzed through the pyramid. We spent hours on that maze program. They've got through it like it was a one-way street.'

'They're not home yet,' reminded Cally. 'They won't solve my codes so quickly.'

She should have added 'I hope'. While their team-mates held off lumbering mummies with sleepshot, Simon Macey and Sonia Dark tested out combinations of hieroglyphics. A single symbol lit up.

'They've got one!' Jennifer cried.

'One's fine. One's okay,' Ben was rationalising furi-ously. 'One doesn't matter. They need all six.'

'Yeah? Well they're halfway there,' observed Jake unhappily, as two further hieroglyphics lit up to give Solo Team hope.

Lori didn't know quite what she should be feeling as she looked on. She was loyal to her friends, of course, and to Ben. She wanted Bond Team to win. But as she watched the intense concentration on Simon's face, she felt that she kind of wanted him to win as well. Whichever way it went, Lori thought, perhaps the real loser would be her.

'Four! That's four symbols,' Eddie observed. 'They only need another two.'

'The math is coming along then, Ed,' commented Jake.

'Another one,' Cally corrected. 'But the code was . . . I don't understand.'

Nobody dared say it when the sixth symbol lit like a good idea. Solo Team whooped in triumph as the Spyscape program terminated. Nobody needed to consult a timepiece. When you've been beaten, you just know it.

'Understand?' Ben had directed his anger and frustration inwards. They infected his words like poison. 'Oh, I think I do. Macey and his mates, they couldn't have done so well so quickly without some kind of help. It's just not possible.'

'What?' Lori said, concerned. 'You think Simon cheated?'

'Worse than that.' Ben regarded the others coldly, clinically. 'I think there's a traitor in Bond Team.'

TWO

'All right, Macey, who was it?' Ben burst into the virtual reality chamber.

'Ben, wait!' With Lori and the rest of Bond Team in pursuit.

The hiss of cyber-cradles opening was still in the air. Simon Macey hadn't even sat up yet, was still wired to the mechanisms that transferred the students between realities. He didn't look like he'd be able to sit up, either. Not with Ben practically on top of him, seizing his collar and shouting.

'Who was it, you cheating scumbag? Who sold us out?'

But Simon Macey was laughing, in a spluttering, half-strangled sort of way. Laughing in Ben's face. 'Second best hard to take, is it, Stanton? Well, get used to it.'

'Ben, let him up. Please.' Lori at one arm, pulling.

Jake at the other. 'Can't you see this is what he wants? You're playing his game.'

'I'd take a step back if I were you, Bond Team.' Sonia Dark and the others were out of their cyber-cradles. They'd brought the instinct for violence from the Spyscape into the virtual reality chamber with them. Shaping up for a fight.

'Or what? A step back or what?' Jennifer for one seemed more than ready to oblige. 'You going to make us?'

'It'll be our pleasure,' said Sonia Dark.

'What—' with a voice like a thunderbolt, Corporal Keene asserted his authority — 'is going on here?'

'I think you could call it a healthy debate, Corporal,' said Eddie.

'Stanton, let go of Macey before I can say Disciplinary Procedures and you find out what they are.' Ben, of course, obeyed, but he didn't like it. 'That's better. Now somebody answer my question. What is going on here?'

'Stanton tried to kill me, sir,' Simon Macey moaned, detaching himself from the cyber-cradle. 'He's a lunatic. Just because we beat them on the Spyscape.'

'You didn't beat us,' Ben raged. 'You cheated. They cheated, Corporal.'

'Is that true, Macey?'

'No, sir. Of course not, sir.' Simon was the definition of the shocked innocent. 'We just did our best like we always do. Stanton's just a bad loser.'

'And do you have any evidence of malpractice on Solo Team's part, Stanton?'

Ben hated to say it but there was no alternative. 'No, sir.'

'Then there's nothing more to be said, is there? Accept the outcome of the competition with the good grace we expect at Deveraux.' Keene stabbed a less than graceful finger at Ben and Simon. 'Now shake hands before I put you both on report.'

'But, sir . . .' Ben was feeling he'd rather cut off his hand than use it to touch Simon Macey.

'Shake.' Keene was unmoved. 'Hands.'

Ben did. He clenched Macey's hand like he wanted to crush it into powder. Simon's grip was just as unforgiving. 'No hard feelings, hey, Stanton?' Simon sneered, though the eyes of both boys reflected plenty of them. 'But I'd calm down a bit if I were you. Be more like Lori. She's the only decent thing about Bond Team.'

And that's when Jake saw everything. He saw Lori's eyes flit to Macey at the mention of her name. He saw the colour rise to her cheeks. He saw her look away again. Guiltily.

'Jake, do you reckon Ben could be right?' Cally asked. 'There couldn't be a traitor in the team, could there? One of us?'

He shook his head firmly. 'No. Don't worry about it, Cal.'

But he kept watching.

'I'm right. I know I am.' Ben prowled the room like a tiger in a cage. 'Somebody has to have passed information about our Spyscape to Macey. There's no other answer.'

Lori watched him nervously. If ever she'd been meaning to tell Ben about Simon's suggestion of a truce, now was not the time. 'But who'd do it, Ben?' she asked, certain that nobody had, and equally sure that Simon would not cheat, though she kept that belief firmly to herself as well. 'And what would they hope to gain? Surely we all want the team to do well.'

'Maybe Daly?' Ben pondered. 'As a way of getting back at me for . . . nah. Stabbing his team-mates in the back isn't his style, even I have to admit that.'

'Of course it isn't.' Lori was genuinely shocked. 'How can you even think it?'

'Cally?' Ben was checking team members off on his fingers. 'We've had our disagreements in the past.'

'Resolved.'

'Maybe Jennifer kind of heard we'd been discussing her behaviour and this is her revenge. Or maybe Eddie . . . nah, it can't be Eddie. That really is ridiculous.'

'It's all ridiculous,' complained Lori, 'and what about me? You haven't accused me yet, Ben. I must be on your list of suspects.'

'What are you talking about?' Ben paused in his pacing and regarded Lori with something in his expression that seemed like hurt. 'I've never doubted you for a second, Lori, not for less time than that. Why do you think I'm talking to you about this? I trust you. Absolutely. You're my girl.'

Lori coloured, hoped that Ben would interpret it as pleasure rather than guilt. 'I'm glad to hear it,' she said, and there was hurt in her voice, too.

Ben sat on the bed beside her, took her hand. 'Listen, I've been meaning to say since we got back from the dome, about the other day, when you called me, you know? I'm sorry I was short with you. I shouldn't have been. I was wrong.'

She didn't hear apologies from Ben very often, admissions of error. Lori felt the need to reciprocate somehow. Maybe now was her chance to say I'm sorry, too, particularly as I went off and got myself snogged by Simon Macey. On the other hand . . . perhaps she should try for something a little less shocking: 'It's all right, Ben. You were on a mission. I was the one being stupid.'

'Makes us well-matched then, doesn't it?' Ben grinned. 'Stupidity is common. Maybe we should get Eddie to make up a threesome.'

'No,' she said. 'I'm happy with just the two of us.'

'Good. Then it's unanimous.' He made to kiss her.

'But, Ben.' Lori pressed a finger to his lips. 'Before we do. This business about Solo Team. Tell me you've changed your mind. Tell me you agree there's no traitor.'

Ben sighed. 'And mean it?' Lori nodded. He sighed again, shrugged defeatedly, in bafflement. 'You're right, Lo. I'm wrong again. There's no traitor. Can't be. But –' and this time it was Ben's finger against Lori's lips – 'Macey got hold of our Spyscape somehow. I'd put money on it.'

'Of course we didn't.' Simon was staggered. 'We want to beat Bond Team, sure, even though you're a member, Lori, but we wouldn't want to cheat to do it. That's unethical. I mean, in the end we'd only be cheating ourselves.'

Lori smiled relievedly. 'I knew as much,' she said. 'I just wanted to hear you say it.'

'Me, I'll say anything you want. So Ben's not too pleased that we've edged ahead, then?' Lori didn't look like she wanted to answer. 'It's all right,' Simon prompted. 'Whatever you say's not going beyond these four walls.' In an environment where privacy was at a premium, Spy High's classrooms were often of greater value to the students empty than when they were hosting lessons. 'Lori?'

'What do you think? We can put the truce idea on ice, at least until after Last Team Standing.' Lori looked away from Simon, remembered herself with Ben only a short time ago. 'And I think we'd better cool it, too, Simon.'

'What? And we were just warming up.'

'I'm Ben's girlfriend, Simon. And I want to be.'

'You sure?' Simon moved back into Lori's line of vision. 'Look me in the eye, Lori.' In The Smile. 'Are you sure? Because you didn't seem quite so clear about it when we kissed. I mean, it was a "we" kind of kiss, wasn't it? Both of us were in there. Maybe if we tried a repeat performance . . .'

Lori shook her head, though with less conviction than she'd been hoping to convey. 'No, Simon, I —'

'Bond Team to Briefing Room One, please.' The tannoy. 'Bond Team to Briefing Room One.'

The students paused, frowned. 'What's that all about?' asked Simon.

Lori shook her head. 'I have no idea, but it means I've got to go and that's probably just as well.'

'I'm not changing the way I feel about you, Lori,' Simon said. 'I know you feel something for me, too. I'll be waiting. When Ben blows it, you know where to find me.'

Lori shifted her weight uncomfortably. 'I've got to go.'

'I'll see you, Lori,' Simon called after her. 'Soon.'

Lori left the classroom at speed, head lowered. She saw Jake's feet just in time to stop herself from colliding with him. Her cry was more in case he should glance past her into the room and observe Simon Macey than for any fear that she might cause him an injury. 'Jake,' she dreaded. 'What are you doing here?'

'Looking for you,' he said simply. 'Seems we've got a briefing to attend.'

'I know.' Lori grabbed Jake's hand and pulled. 'So what are we waiting for?'

She was lucky. Jake followed her and didn't look where she didn't want him to look. Panic over, Lori thought.

Unfortunately for her, Jake hadn't needed to see Simon Macey in the flesh. He'd already heard quite enough.

It was like one of those old war films his dad used to watch on Twentieth Century Gold, Eddie thought. Paratroopers flown in deep behind enemy lines on an ultra-secret mission, parachutes on and sat in two rows staring at each other from either side of the plane, chewing gum and looking mean. Only instead of a plane Bond Team were crammed into the back of a truck that had probably seen service in World War II – everything low-tech, to stop Nemesis snooping – and there wasn't a paratrooper in sight. They were having to make do with

some equally hard-bitten army types brought along by
Keene and ranged opposite the teenagers, and wearing
looks that were so mean Eddie didn't dare catch their
eyes in case they should take offence and enliven the
journey by disembowelling him with their teeth. Keene
sat opposite, too, or at least a working statue of him. The
man with the head of a weasel, introduced as Chief
Interrogator, was up front with the driver and the guy
who was responsible for them all being here in the first
place (wherever 'here' actually was), the former agent of
CHAOS known now as Corbin.

Yep, the likelihood of Eddie being fried by a psychotic
computer virus before bed-time was all down to Corbin.

'Of course,' the voice of Jonathan Deveraux had
said, as his face regarded Bond Team from the screen in
Briefing Room One, 'there is no compulsion on you to
go. Corporal Keene and a platoon of hand-picked men
will accompany you, but even so this operation brings
with it significant risk. That cannot be denied.'

And significant glory, Eddie could almost see Ben
thinking. Significant opportunity to make up for the
Spyscapes.

'We understand, sir,' Ben said in a noble leader sort of
way. 'We want to go.'

'That's right,' Jake echoed.

Eddie wondered why, until he remembered the dome,
Jake's dome, and the destruction that everyone bar
himself and Lori had witnessed first-hand. Back when
he'd been sidelined again. 'We're ready, Mr Deveraux,
sir,' he'd said, though it seemed the room had suddenly
gone deaf.

So here they were. Eddie peered out through the flapping tarpaulin at the back of the truck. He glimpsed ragged trees, a rough track, nowhere in particular. 'Why can't the villains' headquarters ever be anywhere they put in holiday brochures?' he muttered. The truck jolted beneath him. 'Or at least with decent roads. I feel like I've just done twelve rounds with a Turkish masseur.'

'Eddie,' said Cally wearily, 'do the words Shut and Up mean anything to you?'

'More and more each day,' grumbled Eddie, wondering how much more interminable the journey could get. Even an attack by Nemesis would be preferable to death by boredom.

The truck braked. The statue of Keene suddenly became animated and barked orders that only those of a military disposition seemed able to understand. The soldiers clambered out of the truck as one. 'Can't wait for their welcome cocktail,' observed Eddie.

'Come on.' Ben ushered his team-mates. 'We must have arrived.'

It didn't look promising. The track had petered out and in its place a large mound rose before them, like a hill with stunted growth.

'Am I missing the plot here?' Eddie wondered. 'Can CHAOS HQ only be seen with x-ray specs or something?'

'All right, Corbin,' the chief interrogator was advising, 'no tricks.'

Inclining his head slightly to acknowledge the presence of Bond Team, Corbin walked over to a nearby tree, pressed his palm against the trunk and pushed in. At once the mound began to split open, like a mouth smiling a dark and secret smile. The turf, the soil, they were grafted to steel. They became doors. And beyond the doors, a passage, like the entrance to a crypt. Suddenly, being stuck in the truck didn't seem so bad to Eddie.

The same thought had apparently also occurred to Corbin. 'There,' he informed the chief interrogator. 'I've done what I said I'd do. You can find your own way from here. I'll wait in the truck.'

The chief interrogator chuckled. 'The transport stays where it is, Corbin,' he said. 'You don't. Please.' He indicated the gaping fissure in the earth. 'After you.'

It was conceivable at that point that Corbin might have made a break for it had Keene's men not been training their automatic weapons directly on him. He smiled thinly, humourlessly. 'As if they'll be of any use if Nemesis finds us.' Soldiers or guns he didn't specify.

Reluctantly, he moved towards the CHAOS stronghold. 'I want the kids close to me. They've seen what this thing can do.'

'Don't worry, Corbin,' Jake promised, sounding more like a threat. 'We'll be right with you. For the sake of Dome Thirteen.'

Corbin led the way into the complex, Bond Team and the chief interrogator behind him, all of them flanked by Keene and his men, two of whom the corporal posted at the entrance. 'Just in case we need to make a run for it?' Lori whispered to Ben.

The darkness of the earth claimed them.

Torches clicked into life on the soldier's helmets and weapons. The civilian members of the party carried their own, all except Corbin, who seemed to know where he was going even without the benefit of artificial light. Beams of white stabbed into the black, hinting at the presence of hulks of metal, machinery, perhaps, or raw materials, suggesting deep recesses of darkness, unknowable pits and caves where anything could lurk. Eddie found himself hoping that Keene's soldiers were mean in more than expression.

'Wait!' Cally called.

Everybody stopped, bunched up. The tension could almost be tasted behind the spikes of light. 'What is it?' demanded Keene.

'I thought I saw something, out there, something moving in the dark.' But she didn't sound convinced now. 'I thought . . . it looked like a man.'

Corbin laughed hollowly. 'There's nothing moving in here but us, nothing alive. There can't be. Nemesis doesn't leave loose ends.'

'Keep moving, Corbin,' Keene instructed.

'But I saw him, I'm sure,' Cally breathed, to herself more than to Lori, who squeezed her arm encouragingly. 'It was a man, pale as death.'

'The sooner we get out of here the better,' Jennifer muttered. The darkness was too much like her dreams. If it wasn't for the others, for Jake being here, she'd probably be screaming by now. And unable to stop.

'End of the road,' said Corbin, a slab of solid blackness before him. The torches revealed a steel wall and a door. 'The main labs are through here.'

'Then get us in there.' The chief interrogator seemed eager.

'I don't think so.' Corbin shook his head finally. 'The door's fingerprint activated. It won't recognise your signature.'

'It's not our fingerprints it'll be reading.'

'Oh, no. No.' For the first time Corbin seemed genuinely fearful. 'If I use mine and Nemesis is watching, then we're dead. No. If I activate this door I'm killing us all. You can't make me do it!'

'Keene,' said the chief interrogator. 'Show Mr Corbin that we can.'

Keene gestured. Two soldiers grabbed Corbin and forced his left hand against a control panel in the wall. 'No! No! You mustn't!' The man's desperate, almost childish pleas dropped into the darkness like pebbles into a pond, a slight ripple of sound and then gone. 'You've killed us,' Corbin sobbed. 'You've killed us all.'

Bond Team looked at each other uncertainly. If it had been anybody but Corbin, they might have been sympathetic.

The lab door slid open.

'Keep hold of him,' the chief interrogator instructed the soldiers. 'Now, let's see what we can see.' He stepped through the doorway.

Corbin twisted in his captors' grasp to face Bond Team. 'You know what's going to happen now, don't you?' His terrified gaze flitted between them. 'It'll be like the train. We're rats in a trap. Nemesis knows. You understand me? Nemesis is *here*.'

But it didn't seem so. Nobody or nothing living seemed to have been in the lab for a long time. There were banks of computers, rows of control panels, strange technological constructions whose original purpose could only be guessed, but there was not a flicker of electronic activity to any of them. They were smashed, ruined, wrecked. They were debris. It was like a bomb had been detonated in the heart of the lab. Only a faint, faded light lingered in the air, like a ghost. It was at least sufficient for the torches to be turned off. Bond Team returned theirs to their belt pouches.

'Looks like it was one hell of a party,' said Eddie. 'Kind of glad I wasn't invited.' The others looked like they felt the same.

'So this is where Nemesis was born.' The chief interrogator's voice sounded thin and temporary in the lab. 'Let's see if we can find anything we can use. Corbin, with me. I want to know if we can get any of these machines up and running.'

Keene and his soldiers, apart from the two who had manhandled Corbin before and who now seemed permanently assigned to be within grabbing distance of him, spread out to explore the lab further, its dark corners and distant doorways, shunning what feeble light there was.

Corbin himself turned again to Bond Team as if they were some kind of last chance for him. 'Listen, you kids,' he urged, 'I'm relying on you. Talk to him. He has no idea what'll happen to us if we stay here. There's no point us staying. Nemesis has destroyed everything, you can see that. You can see that, can't you?'

'All I can see is a loser who'd have destroyed us if he could,' said Jake, 'and who nearly destroyed my family. Our hearts bleed for you, Corbin.'

'You. Computer girl.' Cally. 'You know what I'm talking about, don't you? You've stopped Nemesis once. It won't forget that. It'll want you. It'll hunt you down.'

'Yeah?' Cally met Corbin's desperate gaze coolly. 'But I reckon it'll want you first.' She hoped her team-mates didn't see her shudder. She remembered the digital eyes, downloading hate, the cybernetic fangs, the computer senses *knowing* who she was.

'Sir? Sir! Over here!' One of the soldiers had found something.

Somebody.

They rushed to his side, encircling a form that had lain unnoticed beneath a collapsed console. The man's lab coat was shredded like bandages, his other clothes the same. Wires like anorexic snakes wound round his limbs, his chest, like ropes binding his body together. More wires noosed his neck and webbed their way over his scalp, his skull.

'What does this mean, Corbin?' demanded the chief interrogator.

Corbin's head shook like a sudden seizure. 'I don't know. I don't . . . it's Patten, one of the virus's . . . fathers . . .'

'Was.' The chief interrogator knelt by the body. 'He's not anything now apart from dead. But what about this?' The interrogator's questing fingers followed the trail of the wires over the dead man's head. They seemed to have burrowed into his skull. The hair was scorched away in several places and the skin blackened and burned. 'Corbin. What's been going on here?'

The chief interrogator raised his head, exposed his Adam's apple as it bobbed in his nervous throat. The dead man's arms shot up like pistons, dead hands clamped around his neck like twin vices. Dead fingers squeezed, powered by more than flesh and blood.

The chief interrogator would be asking no more questions.

'Get back!' Ben cried, yanking Lori with him.

Weapons riddled the disturbingly active body. To a corpse, laser-fire made no difference. Patten got up.

'What did I tell you?' Corbin was screaming. 'We're all going to die!'

'Keep together,' Ben hissed to his team-mates. 'Watch each other's backs.'

'You've got it,' gritted Jake.

A cry from one of the further rooms, a second. Two bursts of laser-fire. Brief. Two soldiers had gone in. Two dead scientists came out, bristling with wires like Patten.

Wires like a puppeteer's strings.

'Nemesis,' gasped Cally. 'It's controlling them.'

'Time to go?' suggested Eddie.

But now the shadows were moving, and closing in. The dead scientists of CHAOS reached for the intruders with pale hands.

'We're surrounded!' someone shouted.

'One hell of a party,' groaned Eddie.

THREE

'Fire at will!' Keene yelled. 'Take them out!'

Laser blasts pulsed into the advancing zombie scientists. The hail of fire staggered them, made them sway as in a strong wind. It slowed them down, but it didn't stop them. The dead kept on coming.

'Form a defensive circle!' snapped Keene. To Bond Team: 'Stay behind us. Stay in the circle.'

'Makes me feel a lot better,' Eddie grunted. 'Anybody remember Custer's Last Stand? Anybody got a plan?'

'How's don't let 'em grab you for a start?' said Jake.

But in an enclosed space, avoiding the homicidal hands of the zombies was easier said than done. The soldier in front of Jennifer was evidently unused to an enemy that would not behave and fall down when shot. He was losing his discipline, drawn forward, breaking the circle. He was focusing so exclusively on one target, that he failed to take account of the others. So they took account of him instead, seizing his arms, twisting them like plasticene, ending the soldier's cries of frustration and fear forever.

Jennifer braced herself as they turned towards her, but they didn't seem to notice, didn't seem to care. The zombies had sightless eyes for only one member of Bond Team, and began to press towards her. Cally.

'Oh, no, you don't, Mr Dead!' Jake swung a metal chair at a zombie's head. The blow shattered its neck and left the head dangling limply, loosely, eyes to the floor. The murderous arms flailed wildly.

And now the uneven battle was well and truly joined. Soldiers and scientists struggled hand to hand, life to death. The integrity of the circle was broken. There was chaos.

'Bond Team, to me!' Keene was trying to protect his students, but Patten seemed to have other ideas and was grappling with the corporal, hands like iron seeking his neck. Only a laser burst at point-blank range jolted the dead man sufficiently for Keene to escape his clutches.

'Think ninja program,' Ben instructed his team-mates. 'Avoid and deflect. Don't let them touch you.'

'They've got one weakness,' Lori added. 'They're slow. We're fast. Make it count.'

Zombie hands lunging. Martial arts techniques knocked them away. Lori was right. If they moved quickly enough, improvised, they could keep at least a temporary advantage. Being dead seemed to slow your reaction times. Bond Team struck out, well-aimed sweeps with their legs sending their attackers crashing awkwardly to the floor, fists and forearms blocking assault after assault. But all the time, growing more tired. And one by one, the soldiers were falling.

'Cally!' Jennifer tried to make herself heard above the cries and clamour. 'They want Cally!'

'I didn't know I was so popular,' Cally observed, dodging and then kicking to send her newest assailant toppling, 'but I could do with some help here.'

Bond Team closed ranks.

'Nemesis knows you're the biggest ,threat,' Jake realised. 'You stopped it on the train. It thinks you might be able to stop it now.'

'And Cal,' moaned Eddie, a flurry of blows beating back a zombie, 'we kind of hope so too.' Dead fingers brushed his shoulder. 'And make it quick, yeah?'

Corbin didn't plan on waiting. His fear had become cunning now, the survival instinct of the trapped animal. When the two soldiers guarding him became embroiled in the rather more pressing matter of saving their own lives, he saw his chance. Just for a moment, the ebb and flow of conflict had opened a path to the lab door. Corbin darted for it.

He scarcely expected to get there but he did. Now he could turn the tables on the lot of them, his deceased former comrades, those brainless soldiers, those annoying kids, all of them. 'Corbin!' The corporal was shouting after him. Well, let him shout. Use the old vocal chords while he could, before they were ripped out like string. Corbin waved farewell and slipped out of the lab.

The door was fingerprint activated. He'd told them that. And he'd warned them, too, but they'd forced him to open it. Nobody had to force him to close it again. Everyone else would stay inside.

But what about him? Not safe yet. Plenty of darkness out here for the dead to hide in. Not safe yet.

Corbin ran, raced towards the distant prospect of freedom and the outside world. Ahead of him, the wide open doors of the complex itself, the light at the end of a particularly unsettling tunnel.

At every gasping, whimpering, heart- and foot-pounding metre of the way, Corbin expected white hands to thrust out of blackness, to grasp him and twist him and break him into pieces. But it didn't happen. Nemesis must have concentrated its focus on the lab itself. Almost howling with elated relief, Corbin burst out into reassuring sunlight and the blithe trill of birdsong.

The absence of the soldiers Keene had posted at the complex's entrance did not seem to occur to Corbin. There was room in his overwrought mind for one thought only.

The truck. Because the truck meant escape. The truck meant safety.

He hugged himself with delight. There was the truck. Here he was clambering into the driver's seat. There were the keys, conveniently still in the ignition. Not that he'd needed the keys. He could have hotwired the truck. He was Corbin, agent of CHAOS. He could do anything. He turned the key: the truck's engine fired first time. Maybe he'd even relaunch the organi-sation, this time with himself as undisputed leader, of course. He was alive and he was safe and anything was possible.

Only next time there wouldn't be a Nemesis. Too dan-gerous. Too unpredictable. He wondered whether those strange, intense kids were dead yet. No, next time there'd be no mistakes, and no loose ends.

Like the soldiers at the entrance. Corbin remembered them now. Where had they gone?

Maybe in the truck. Maybe that was them moving about behind him.

The sweat on his skin turned to ice.

Maybe it wasn't.

Corbin froze. He didn't dare look behind him.

Until a pair of dead, white hands seized his head and turned it round for him. All the way round.

They couldn't last much longer. Cally knew it as well as the others, as well as the soldiers who were being overwhelmed by their apparently unstoppable assailants with increasing regularity. The shrinking band of survivors' backs were against the wall – literally as well as metaphorically. Even the zombies seemed to sense that their triumph was only a matter of time.

If only they could break that control, Cally thought, disrupt it somehow. But 'somehow' wasn't going to be good enough. If only she had time to plan, to come up with an idea. But time wasn't on their side, either.

'Cal!' someone shouted.

Behind her. She wheeled but hands like cold meat were on her, clamped around her throat. It was Patten, forcing her down. She couldn't dislodge him.

'Help me!' Cally choked out her appeal. 'Some . . . one . . . help . . .'

Patten was squeezing at her throat like it was a tube of toothpaste. She heard her neck cracking.

'Some . . . one . . .' The world was turning dark.

And then came a message for her from beyond the grave. It was Patten's voice, but another's words: 'Organic . . . forms . . . im . . . pure . . .'

And there seemed to be a gleam of sadistic pleasure in the scientist's eyes, those staring zombie eyes only inches away now from her own. A gleam that throbbed and pulsated like a yellow heartbeat. And not *in* the eyes, either, but *behind* them. Behind them.

No way could Cally afford to die now. The others were relying on her.

She clung to consciousness like a drowning man to a lifebelt. Keene – was it Keene? – was battering Patten's skull impotently, splintering it like a treetrunk. 'Eyes,' Cally croaked. 'Behind the eyes . . . Shoot . . .'

Keene got the point. There was a blinding flash by her face and a savage thunder of noise. Patten jolted backwards, his capacity for vision reduced by half. He released his hold and Cally gasped for air. Through the hole where his eyeball had been, brains and circuits mingled uselessly. Dead again.

'Control chip,' Cally coughed. 'That's the answer.'

'The eyes!' Keene cried out, like Archimedes inspired. 'Aim for the eyes!'

As if they understood the corporal's words, and maybe they did, Patten's fellow zombies momentarily paused, almost seemed to glance at each other for advice. The surviving soldiers didn't pause, momentarily or any other way. They took aim. They fired.

Eyeballs popped like champagne corks.

And the zombies fell, as if struck by a sudden desire to be buried, a sudden realisation that the dead had no right to be attacking the living like this. As if the puppets' strings had suddenly been snipped.

A roar of hope from the remaining humans. The tide was turning.

'Great shooting, guys,' admired Eddie. 'Looks like you win the whole row of kewpie dolls.'

'Cal, are you okay?' Jennifer and Jake were kneeling by her, helping her into a sitting position.

'I've been,' she managed hoarsely, 'better.'

'You've done well, Cross,' Keene approved. 'All of you. I think we have the situation well in hand now.'

The lab floor was littered with the bodies of the zombies, not to mention the chief interrogator and the majority of Keene's men.

'Hey, Corbin's gone,' Ben realised. 'And he's shut us in.'

'Don't fret, Stanton,' said Keene. 'He won't get far.'

'Neither will we, Corporal,' Ben pointed out. 'We need Corbin's fingerprints to open the door.'

'Ben . . . it's all . . . right . . .' Cally felt like she was talking through a mangle. 'The other . . . scientists . . . must have had access . . . too . . .'

'The other scientists?'

Cally indicated the heaps of white-coated bodies. 'Take . . . your pick.'

It was a weary and generally disheartened Bond Team who finally returned with Corporal Keene to Spy High. They'd found Corbin's corpse in the truck, as well as two others who'd had to come eye to eye with a laser bolt in order to remind them of the fact. But the entire ill-fated expedition to CHAOS' last laboratory complex had yielded no significant new intelligence, granted no hint as to how to locate and eliminate Nemesis. All it had done was lose lives.

'That's the risk we all take in this line of work,' Keene said on the journey home. 'Be grateful they weren't yours.' Eddie wondered why the corporal didn't go in for motivational speaking.

'Shower and sleep,' Ben groaned, as they ached their way towards their rooms. 'And maybe both at the same time.'

'Think I could do with a drink or something first,' said Jennifer. 'Anyone fancy joining me? Jake?' With pointed hopefulness.

Jake seemed torn. 'No, I don't think so, Jen. Sorry. Think I'll just turn in as well.'

'Oh.' Jennifer tried hard to mask her disappointment, but wondered if Jake really fancied her as much as Cally said he did, wouldn't he have said yes in order to spend time with her? 'Okay. It doesn't matter.' The others didn't seem interested, either. 'Just me, then.'

'Nah, can't have that. I'll keep you company, Jen,' Eddie volunteered.

'Great, Eddie. Thanks.' Jennifer saw Cally raise her eyebrows sympathetically. And it may have been tiredness or stress blurring her vision, but just as she and Eddie left the others to make for the rec room, Jennifer thought she also saw Jake lightly touching Lori's shoulder, softly whispering something in her ear. But she must have imagined that. What would Jake want with Lori that seemed so secretive?

Lori herself asked the same question after lying to Ben and Cally that she and Jake had decided to grab a drink after all. They never got as far as the rec room. The studies at Deveraux were as effective at hosting confrontations as they were at being elevators.

'Well, Mr Secret and Urgent?' Lori could see that something was bothering Jake. 'What's the matter? This isn't like you, Jake.'

'Consorting with the enemy's not like you either, Lori, but it's happening, isn't it?'

'What? What do you mean?' For several seconds of disbelieving silence on Jake's part, Lori really couldn't guess. Her definition of enemy took a while to expand far enough to include Simon Macey. But when it did, she knew exactly what Jake meant. She was in trouble. 'I don't understand,' she bluffed awkwardly. 'Maybe I'd better just . . .' Lori headed for the door.

'Simon Macey,' said Jake, stopping her in her tracks like the words were some sort of paralysis spell. 'Tell me about you and Simon Macey, Lori.'

'Jake?' Lori half-turned towards him, but didn't trust a direct gaze. 'There isn't a me and Simon Macey. How could there be?'

'I don't know, Lori,' mused Jake, 'but there was I thinking Ben had gone off the deep end again with all his rant about a traitor in the team, you know, just as a kind of cover-up story to excuse the fact that we'd been beaten for once, and there was I more than half expecting our noble leader to accuse me of being in league with

Macey, and then, what do I discover?' his voice becoming colder, flintier. 'There is a traitor after all, and it's not me. It's you, Lori.'

'I'm not a traitor, Jake.' Lori's blue eyes flashed denial at that. 'You're wrong.'

'Lori,' Jake sighed, 'I saw your reaction after the Spyscaping. I heard you with Macey in the classroom before we went off with Keene.'

Lori shook her head. 'I don't know what you're talking about.'

'Lori, I'm not imaginative enough to make this up,' Jake persisted. 'I mean, I heard what you said, the both of you. He's not changing the way he feels. He knows you feel something for him, too. I mean, tell me I'm making this up.'

'You're making it up.' But she spoke to the floor.

'So you haven't been secretly seeing Simon Macey? Haven't been passing him information about our Spyscape and who knows what else?'

'No. No. No. You're wrong, Jake.' But her body language said right. 'And I think we're finished here.'

'I could have gone straight to Ben with this.' Jake tried a different approach. 'I could have told him without speaking to you, Lori. Doesn't that suggest something? I only want to help. Ben's right about one thing. You can't trust Simon Macey.'

You can, Lori thought. If only the others realised that. 'I don't need any help, Jake.'

He was losing her. She was at the door. 'I could still do it,' he warned. 'I could go and tell Ben right now. Is that what you want, Lori?'

'Jake,' she said, 'you do whatever you like.' And she closed the door behind her.

So why didn't he, then? Go to Ben. It'd be a crushing blow to the Stanton ego, learning that the girlfriend whose loyalty and talents he'd been boasting about to Jake before was in fact the traitor and in Simon Macey's pocket, if not elsewhere about his person. It'd be a rich revenge for all Ben's insults.

But revenge didn't help the team, didn't boost morale. Revenge was for the bitter. He couldn't tell Ben or anyone else, even though it was obvious Lori was lying. But Jake couldn't quite bring himself to believe that she was cold-bloodedly selling them out, either. Not Lori. She was too – he groped for the right word – good.

Still, he couldn't let the matter rest like this. He had to do something.

Jake sighed. Seemed his bed would have to wait a while yet.

Eddie and Ben were sound asleep. It'd probably take Nemesis smashing through the wall to make either of them stir, and then they'd be likely simply to turn over on their other side. Even so, Jake applied the clingskin as quietly as possible, then whispered the window open as wide as it would go.

He didn't want to put his foot through the glass on his way out.

Not as sheer as the Wall, not actually moving like the Light Train, clingskinning up and down the exterior of the Deveraux College was going to be a doddle. Jake kept his concentration levels high, however. Falling three floors into the shrubbery would be an embarrassing way to break your neck.

He slithered along the wall between the rows of windows, keeping well out of range of anyone who was still up and might want to take an admiring peek at the night. Lovers, maybe. Or conspirators.

Jake knew the location of Simon Macey's room. He counted the number of windows along from his own. Didn't want to snoop on just anybody. When he'd activated his belt-mic and inserted his ear-piece, he was no longer certain he even wanted to eavesdrop on Simon Macey. The belt-mic could record a heartbeat through a metre of concrete. It brought the slobbering sounds of Macey and Sonia Dark distressingly close for comfort. Still, he supposed he ought to count his blessings: at least he didn't have to watch.

Jake shifted his weight and would have sighed had the making of any sound while clinging to a wall outside someone's window not been a bad idea. He was wasting his time. He'd hoped that if the room was empty he'd have been able to slip in and find evidence of Macey's involvement with Lori – some proof to challenge her with. Alternatively, he'd hoped that he'd catch Macey saying something incriminating, thinking he was safe from prying ears. Neither possibility was working out, and if he had to listen to Simon and Sonia's game of tonsil hockey for very much longer his dinner would be vacating his stomach.

Relief at last. Permanent, Jake prayed. Macey was laughing, the way con-artists must do when they trick old ladies. 'What's so funny?' Sonia Dark was saying. Jake's question too.

'Just thinking of Stanton's expression again. Priceless. If it was a photograph I'd have it framed.'

'Really?' Sonia Dark didn't sound entirely impressed. 'Sometimes, Simon, I think your rivalry with Ben Stanton is more important to you than I am.'

'Then sometimes you're wrong, babe.'

No making up, Jake begged silently. Please, no making up.

'Really?' Sonia repeated, unconvinced. 'Well I think you're taking too great an interest in Lori Angel.' Maybe Jake's little clingskin excursion wasn't going to be a total loss, after all. 'I know what you said, but it looks to me like you're beginning to enjoy being with her.'

'I am,' Simon admitted, 'all the while she's useful to us. I mean, getting her password for the Spyscapes was a bit of all right, wasn't it? Bit of a sneak preview didn't do us any harm, did it? And there'll be more to come yet, plenty more information I'll be able to squeeze out of her.'

'It's the squeezing part that worries me.'

'It shouldn't.' A wet slap of a kiss. Jake wondered if he'd heard enough. 'We all have to make sacrifices for the cause, and mine is having to tolerate a brainless bimbo like Lori. But don't worry. It'll only be until after Last Team Standing, then I think someone had better tell Stanton exactly what his precious blue-eyed babe has been up to, don't you? All in the spirit of comradeship and unity, of course.'

More laughter. Jake almost preferred the smooching.

'So you really don't like her, Simon?'

'Haven't I already said? All right, one more time.'

It was probably as well that Simon Macey couldn't see Jake's expression during the one more time. He wouldn't have slept that night. Jake's anger was cold inside him, like an iceberg. Macey was more of a sleaze than he could have predicted. Lori was being manipulated and she didn't even know it. He obviously couldn't tell Ben. It was going to be down to him to do something to rescue the situation.

The only question was what.

FOUR

Today was the day. She couldn't wait any longer. She had to be sure. After all, what advice had Cally given her? *'All you've got to do about it is go up to him and say hi . . . Talk to him. Tell him how you feel.'* It was advice Jennifer finally felt ready to take. The dreams still haunted her sleep, prowled her nights, but they were less painful now, as was always the case once the anniversary had passed for another year. Her mind was clearer and she was able to give thought to other dreams – the future instead of the past. She, Jake and the others had survived a second encounter with Nemesis. They'd been given time off their studies to recover from the ordeal at the CHAOS complex. So the timing was perfect. There would be no better opportunity.

Today was the day.

Lori and Cally had already left their room before Jennifer had built her courage sufficiently to follow their example. She didn't feel like breakfast. She didn't feel like anything much until she'd established once and for all if there was a Jennifer and Jake on the emotional horizon. She made straight for the boys' room, knocked, hoped Jake would answer. *He'd answer and she'd say 'hi' and he'd know what she meant and he'd say 'hi' back and they'd be together and they'd talk . . .*

'Lori, is that . . .?' The door opened. 'Jennifer?'

'Ben?' And still in his pyjamas.

Two disappointed and slightly puzzled members of Bond Team stared at each other.

'Sorry, I was expecting Lori.' Ben grinned sheepishly. 'We said we'd . . . you know, spend some quality time. Kind of, like, together. Is she still . . .?' He thumbed vaguely towards the girl's accommodation wing.

'Actually, no,' said Jennifer. 'I haven't seen her.' And why did that single statement of fact suddenly seem suspicious?

'Oh, okay.' Ben didn't appear to mind. 'Are you . . . did you . . .?'

'Jake,' Jennifer announced. 'Can I see Jake?'

'What for?' Was that a knowing grin? Was Ben teasing her?

'What, I need to fill out a form or something before I can see a team-mate?' If he was teasing, he'd soon be doing it from the horizontal.

'No,' said Ben curiously, 'but you'll need pretty good eyes if you want to see him from there. Jake's not here. It's just me, I'm afraid.'

'Oh.' Don't give up, Jennifer forced herself. Today was the day. 'Do you know where . . .?'

Ben shook his head. 'Sorry, no idea. I'd invite you in to wait for him, Jen, but I need to get dressed before Lori comes.'

'Sure,' Jennifer said. 'You don't want to put her off.'

So not a good start. She wandered along the corridors. Jake not around, and no Lori, either, as if that meant something. Maybe they were eating breakfast. Separately, she hoped, or at the same table but only because they were members of the same team and not because they were holding hands or anything.

She was right. They weren't holding hands. But they were together. With a sudden intake of breath, Jennifer saw them from the window – Lori and Jake, in the grounds outside the school.

He was being earnest with her, urging, pleading. His hands were wanting to touch her. She was shaking her head, trying to ignore him, look away. Until he said something else and there was a moment of total stillness. Until he ended it by resting his hands tenderly on her shoulders. Until she nodded, accepted him, tearfully. Until they moved off together and Jennifer could not see where they went.

It had been like a mime show or a silent movie, the kind of entertainment that requires no words to communicate meaning. Jennifer interpreted for herself. This was the last time she'd listen to Cally's advice. So much for today being the day. The only day that truly mattered in Jennifer's life had been years ago, and its consequences were still at work within her. The thought of Jake had been a distraction from them, a delusion. A promise broken like all the others.

She'd go to the holo-gym on her own. Combat program. Preparation. She'd fight.

She didn't need Jake anyway.

Jennifer Chen didn't need anybody.

Eddie dug his toes into the white sand, stretched lavishly and luxuriated in the blazing Caribbean sun. 'This is the life, isn't it, Cal?' He rolled onto his side and winked at Cally who was spread out on the beach alongside him. She didn't deny it. Eddie let his gaze wander over the perfect palm-fringed bay: the clear calm waters of the sea sparkled invitingly just metres away, and there wasn't another human being in sight. He and Cally had paradise all to themselves. 'As good as the real thing, this. Only problem is, you don't get to take your tan back into the real world with you.'

'I can live with it,' said Cally with her eyes closed.

'You're sounding better today,' Eddie remarked. 'No long-term injury to the voice, then, Cally?'

'Apparently not,' Cally replied, 'though if you keep going on, Eddie, the same might not apply to my ears.'

'Sorry.' Eddie rolled onto his back again, squinting at the sky through his sunglasses. 'Peace and quiet, rest and relaxation, that's what this leisure program's all about. Thought you'd like it. That's why I suggested you join me, Cal.'

'I'm grateful, Eddie. Really.'

'Actually—' this time Eddie sat up, hunched forward, and cast a faintly embarrassed glance in Cally's direction — 'to be honest with you, Cal, that wasn't the only reason.'

Cally opened her eyes. 'If you're thinking about any funny business, Eddie, *don't* think about it. Skinny-dipping's out for a start.'

'No, Cal.' Eddie sounded hurt. 'Nothing like that. Though we did have a good time at Christmas, didn't we? I mean, I know I did.'

'I know you did, too,' Cally grunted, 'but Christmas was a one-off, Eddie. Compliments of the season. Nothing serious. I thought we both realised that. I like you as a friend, but—'

'Forget about the but,' Eddie said. 'Friend is good enough, 'cause what I really wanted to do this morning was to talk to you, Cal. As a friend.'

'Yeah?' Intrigued, Cally sat up, too. First Jennifer, now Eddie. Seemed like she was kick-starting a career as Bond Team's Agony Aunt. 'Okay, you have my undivided attention, Eddie. Shoot.'

'Do you think I pull my weight in this team, Cal?'

Cally considered. 'It depends, Eddie. How much do you weigh?'

'No, I mean seriously.' Eddie sighed and shrugged like someone defeated. 'That's exactly what I mean. You don't take me seriously, no one does. Why does everyone treat me like the team idiot?'

'Because you're always acting like it?' Cally suggested. 'It's the way you come across, Eddie, you must know that. More like a stand-up comedian than a secret agent.'

'So you don't think I am pulling my weight?'

'I didn't say that. It's just your personality.'

'Great. Just my personality.' Eddie frowned forlornly.

'You know, when we signed up for Deveraux I was sure I was going to make my mark. I was going to be the spy with the smile. And since then I've come so far bottom in every class my marks'll soon start coming back wearing pants. I've been surplus to requirements fighting Frankenstein and left behind to twiddle my thumbs while the rest of you go off to Jake's dome. Seems to me like it's too much smile and not enough spy.'

'Being a bit hard on yourself, Eddie, aren't you?' Cally raised her sunglasses and regarded Eddie sympathetically. 'Listen, I didn't think that I fitted in too well at Spy High last term. Ben in particular was giving me a bad time, remember? But you've got to have faith, in yourself, in your abilities. Doubt's natural. It's how you get through it that makes you strong. And for what it's worth, I like you just the way you are. I wouldn't want you to change at all.'

'No?' Eddie seemed to cheer up a little. 'Not even a bit more muscle on the old biceps?'

Cally grinned. 'There's enough intensity on the team from some of the others. We need a joker in the pack, someone who can keep us sane when the world seems to be falling apart. That's your job, Eddie, and nobody does it as well as you.'

'Ah, you're just saying that, Cal.'

False modesty now. Eddie was rapidly approaching normal again. Cally thought she'd give him one last encouragement. 'No, it's the truth. And you might not believe this either, Eddie, but when we're in danger there's no one I'd sooner have at my back.'

'Yeah? Well I'm pretty cool with you being at my front, too, Cal. Maybe we could kind of practise some positioning now, 'cause in this place you never know when we might need to go into action.'

'Down, tiger,' laughed Cally. 'I think we're pretty safe here, unless a couple of ninjas go AWOL from the combat programs.'

In the distance, far beyond the blue horizon, there was a flicker and a rumble.

'Sounds like they heard you, Cal.'

'It's only a storm, Eddie.'

Blackness spilled like an oil-slick across the sky, tainting and polluting.

'Yeah, well I've got a bit of a problem with that, Cal,' Eddie said, removing his sunglasses and dropping them by his side. 'There aren't supposed to be any storms in this program, not even a spit of rain.' He got to his feet, warily gazing out to a sea that was no longer calm, no longer tranquil.

'So what do you call that?' Cally joined him, slipped her hand into his.

Blackness billowed towards them.

'I call it trouble,' said Eddie.

'We all have to make sacrifices for the cause, and mine is having to tolerate a brainless bimbo like Lori.'

Lori winced, ashen-faced. Each word was like a slap. Simon's voice might have been reduced in volume now that it was issuing from Jake's belt-recorder, but its impact was as great as if he was bellowing in her ear.

Brainless bimbo . . .

The worst thing was, he was right. She'd been so easy to deceive, to dupe. The Smile. It hadn't been real. Lori hung her head in shame and humiliation.

'. . . worry. It'll only be until after Last Team Standing, then . . .'

'Jake, please.' Meekly, defeatedly. 'No more.'

Jake clicked off the recorder and slotted it back into his belt. 'Talk to me, Lori,' he said. 'How did it happen?'

Lori sighed deeply. She gazed out of the window, her expression distant and lost. 'Simon approached me after you'd gone to the dome,' she admitted. 'He was charming, attentive. He made me feel important, valued, and I've always wanted to feel that, Jake, I need to feel valued. And Ben leaving me behind like he did, taking Jennifer . . . I guess I was a little insecure. I let my defences down. And he started by assuring me he wanted to make peace between our two teams. And I believed him. I believed everything he said, Jake, even though Ben had told me to watch him. How gullible is that? Makes you want to laugh, doesn't it?'

'I'm not laughing,' Jake said, 'and I'm not blaming you, Lori. Wanting to see the best in people, that's better than wanting to see the worst.'

Lori's lips twitched feelingly and bitterly. 'Better for who? So anyway, Jake, you've found the traitor. Ben was right all along. Thanks to me, we can probably say goodbye to the Sherlock Shield and I can certainly say goodbye to a boyfriend. Ben's not going to find this easy to forgive.'

Jake cast Lori a 'more fool him' look, followed it up more positively. 'Ben doesn't have to know.'

'What do you mean? You're not going to tell him?'

'Why would I tell him? What good would that do?'

'But what about Simon? What's to stop him . . .?'

Jake dismissed the idea. 'He's not going to be telling Ben anything while he thinks you don't know the truth, Lori. You heard him on the tape. Our friend Simon's not finished with you yet.'

'Oh, yes, he is,' Lori suddenly blazed, her dismay finding an outlet in rage. 'I'd sooner cuddle up to Stromfeld than go near Simon Macey again.'

'No, no, Lori,' mused Jake. 'Let's not be too hasty.'

'Too what?'

'Macey doesn't know I taped him. We've got the advantage now, and maybe there's some way we can use it.' Jake smiled conspiratorially at Lori. 'Know what I mean?'

'I'm beginning to.' Lori returned Jake's smile.

'Maybe there's some way we can turn the tables on Simon Macey and Solo Team.'

The temperature was dropping alarmingly. Clad only in their swimming costumes Cally and Eddie were beginning to shiver uncontrollably. And now it was as if night had fallen, the deepest, darkest night of the year. Paradise was poisoned.

'Correction,' said Eddie. 'I make this Big Trouble. Let's leave it for the techs to sort out. Voice ID Nelligan: end program.'

'Voice ID Cross: end program.'

And that would be it, of course. Ending the program would initiate a safe, swift transfer from the virtual world to the cyber-cradles at Spy High where the students' flesh and blood bodies patiently awaited their minds' return, immune from harm. The system was perfect. Nothing could go wrong. A second for the transference mechanism to activate.

Wind struck Cally and Eddie head-on, like a battering ram, knocking them backwards across the sand. But the wind was not the greatest shock.

'It's not working!' Cally cried. 'End program! Voice ID Cross: end program!'

'Try End program please,' suggested Eddie, scrabbling to his feet again. He stared up at the thundering peaks of the sky. White lights sparked and crackled like electricity. 'I've got a feeling someone doesn't like us.'

A lightning bolt daggered from above, directly at them. Astonished by the quickness of his own reflexes, Eddie threw himself and Cally out of its path. The beach combusted where they'd been, atomising Eddie's abandoned sunglasses.

'Put my mind at ease, Cal,' he urged. 'Tell me what's happening.'

'Something's overridden the program.' Eddie didn't like the look in Cally's eyes. 'Something hostile. Something that doesn't want us to leave.'

'Can I guess yet?'

A second bolt of lightning split the nearest palm tree asunder, sending flames shooting into the air. And the dark clouds above were rotating now, spinning and spiralling in a dizzy, whirling pattern as the ground began to shake.

'Nemesis.' Cally hissed the name. 'It knows we're here. It's coming for me, Eddie.' She held on to him tightly.

'Yeah? Well it's not going to get you.' He tried to sound confident. The spy with a smile. 'Not with Eddie Nelligan at your back, remember? Come on.' He dragged her towards the pitiful cover of the palms. 'And think, Cal. There's got to be a way out. There's got to be a back-up procedure in case of system breakdown, hasn't there?'

'You're right.' Cally nodded, tried to think straight. (*'Organic . . . forms . . . im . . . pure'*) Tried to forget that, and the strangling hands of zombie scientists. It wasn't easy. 'Maybe the techs back in the chamber . . . they'll know something's wrong . . .' But she'd been stupid, stupid to allow Eddie to persuade her here. She should have realised, should have known better. But she'd been tired. She hadn't thought. In the virtual world, Nemesis was the hunter. And Cally had just made herself prey.

There was a whirlpool in the sky. At its centre, a single, staring eye. A beam like a searchlight stabbed from it, prowled across the ravaged beach, towards the palm trees.

Eddie dragged Cally deeper into the undergrowth. 'Listen, we'll be all right,' he promised. 'We can't be harmed in here anyway, can we? I mean, this is only virtual reality, right? Our physical bodies are perfectly safe, right, Cal?'

The light beam probed through the foliage, closing in on the students inexorably, inevitably. The vortex in the sky seemed to be building to some violent crescendo.

'If only.' Eddie stumbled and Cally almost fell over him. She gripped his shoulder, had to make him understand the peril of their situation. 'It's our minds that matter, Eddie, our minds that are sending signals back to our bodies. And our minds believe this is real.'

'So if we believe we're hurt . . .' Eddie's heart chilled with understanding.

'Nemesis will have overridden the safety protocols. Eddie, if we die here, we'll die for real.'

'Im . . . pure . . .'

Both students screamed as pain raked across their minds like claws. The voice of Nemesis was like fingernails scraping on a blackboard, piercing, screeching.

'Organic . . . forms . . . impure . . .'

The words were not spoken aloud. They were in the teenagers' heads, like broken glass in their brains.

And now the light had found them, stripping away their flimsy cover. Cally was dazzled, her skull on fire and every limb aching. She couldn't see perfectly what happened next, which was probably just as well.

The sky split open and midnight rain splattered the students like old blood. The vortex gaped like a rotting mouth. Something forced its way through, something that glittered darkly and pulsated with power.

Cally had glimpsed the face of Nemesis before, its bulging black eyes and the cold, computerised codes behind them, its robot maw and the electrodes within, its digital glare of hatred. But now its spider's legs, like spiked steel pylons, like gleaming metal girders, prodded from the vortex and sought purchase on the sand of the beach. The jagged, machine body followed, the head, the glinting, calculating eyes, the electrode fangs that sparked with deadly current, and finally the swollen, crackling abdomen, its cyber-circuits encased in chitinous armour. The corruption was here. The virus had arrived.

Nemesis towered above the students, fixed them with an implacable stare.

'Organic forms . . . impure . . . eradicate . . .'

'Not what you'd call a conversationalist,' muttered Eddie. 'Come on, Cal.'

If he was looking for an escape route, the options were suddenly reduced. The ground rumbled and then erupted – great pillars of stone hammered up through the soil to hem them in. Nemesis seemed to nod its approval.

'It's remaking the landscape,' Cally gasped, 'reprogramming in its own image. There's nothing we can do!' As Nemesis bore down upon them. 'Eddie, I don't know what to do!'

No jokes now. No time. Eddie placed himself between Cally and Nemesis. 'Run, Cal! Get as far as you can! I'll hold it off!' With what, would have been a good question. Eddie doubted that courage alone would impress the virus.

With a speed which belied its size, Nemesis' head lunged down and forward, inspecting Eddie like an insect. Instinctively, Eddie threw up his arms to protect himself. The mouth would close on him and he'd be fried. The current generated by the twin electrodes would cook his internal organs and peel the flesh from his bones like old wallpaper.

He closed his eyes before the end, screamed out '*No!*'

And there was darkness, true, but no pain. Maybe death had got a bad press.

Then there were hands on him, human hands, and Eddie realised that he wasn't dead and that was good, and he wasn't in the virtual reality program any more either, and that was even better. He was in his cyber-cradle. The technical assistants were disconnecting him. 'Get him free,' someone was urging, 'while we've still got control.'

'Cally,' Eddie demanded. 'What about Cally?'

He tried to pull himself out of the cyber-cradle but was too weak. His head spun and the prospect of being violently sick was imminent. The techs supported him, eased him out. 'Steady, Nelligan. Take it slowly. You've survived an ordeal. Just relax.'

'Relax?' The word seemed to have no meaning. 'Where's Cally? Is she all right?'

The techs exchanged anxious glances. That was a no, then. Eddie snapped his gaze to Cally's cyber-cradle. It was surrounded by more technical assistants. They were silent, like mourners at a funeral.

'Cally!' Eddie lurched drunkenly towards her cradle. 'What's the matter with her? What's going on?' The techs parted and let him through. 'Cally? Oh, no . . .'

She might have been sleeping. Her expression was calm, her body at peace, but her mind, that was elsewhere. In a virtual world of its own design, Nemesis evidently still had some use for Cally. She wasn't dead, but she wasn't truly alive, either.

Cally was in a coma.

FIVE

'**W**e can keep her body functioning like this indefinitely,' said the tech. 'We can feed her nourishment, prevent the muscles from atrophying with physiotherapy. She could remain like this for the rest of her natural life.'

Sleeping, but not sleeping. Unconscious, but not really that, either. Lacking consciousness, which was different. Lacking a mind. Lacking a soul. The shell of Cally Cross, the memory of her, empty and hollow. Bond Team, the tech and Senior Tutor Grant were gathered hushedly at her cyber-cradle. That was wrong now, too, Lori thought, the name. A cradle suggested birth, new life. The receptacle in which Cally's body was stored was more like a coffin now, a coffin with a glass lid, like the one in which the poisoned Snow White lay before she was raised again by the prince. Who was there here to be Cally's prince? Who could bring her back to life?

'What about her mind?' Lori asked, praying for miracles. 'How can we restore it?'

The tech shuffled embarrassedly, looked at no one. 'I've told you what we can do,' he said. 'Returning Cally's consciousness to her is the one thing we cannot. From what Eddie's told us, we must assume that somehow her mind, her personality, her essence, if you will, is stranded in the cyber-world, and at the mercy of Nemesis.'

'Then we've got to get it out.' The solution seemed straightforward to Jake. 'Or go in after her. We can't just do nothing, stand around and do nothing.'

'Cally's one of us,' Ben echoed. 'Whatever it takes, we'll do it.'

Jennifer and Lori assented. Eddie mumbled and wished he was in the cradle instead of Cally. Was he imagining it, or were the eyes of the others closed against him, their comments somehow directed at him? Like veiled accusations with the sub-text: why had he allowed Cally to be claimed by Nemesis? Why hadn't he made a stand? And the bottom line: why was he here without her? Bond Team stood or fell together. And while his team-mates didn't say these things aloud, Eddie knew they were thinking them. His team-mates thought he was a failure.

And why not? They were right, weren't they? He'd failed Cally, hadn't he? And he didn't dare tell them what he realised now had happened at the end. With Nemesis poised to strike, Eddie had expected only death. But the virus hadn't killed him. It had simply sent him away, back to the world of flesh and blood and regret. Nemesis had not even deemed him to be worthy of death. Nemesis had dismissed him, like he was nothing. *Nothing.* Seemed Nemesis was a good judge of character.

Jennifer was making a suggestion, albeit a suicidal one. Her eyes were blazing. 'Can't we be sent into the program? We can fight Nemesis, bring Cally back. She's alive in there, isn't she? It's not too late?'

'No, her consciousness is unimpaired,' admitted the tech. 'If it was damaged to any life-threatening extent, her vital signs would be affected. But as far as being too late, I'm afraid that's more difficult to determine. If Cally's mind is suffering sustained mental trauma, which we have to concede may be likely, then the consequences for her health if . . . *when* her mind is returned to her body, well, they could be considerable.'

'What do you mean?' Lori said.

'Brain damage,' the tech winced. 'Severe brain damage.'

'Then what are we waiting for?' Jennifer seemed already to be picking her cyber-cradle.

Grant raised his hands like he was surrendering, maybe to the inevitable. 'Hold on a minute. Jennifer. All of you. Wait.'

'For what?' Jake resented. 'Nemesis to finish Cally off?'

'For orders. For your Senior Tutor to decide what to do.' Grant pulled rank. 'Now I know you want to help Cally. We all do. But sending anybody into virtual reality at this point, with Nemesis infecting the system, would be effectively to sign their death warrant. Mr Deveraux has ordered a total closedown of all computer systems in the college, apart from those that provide the most vital services, such as Cally's life support here, for the duration of this crisis. Our first priority must be to strengthen our security programs and to defend the integrity of our so far unviolated systems.' Grant regarded his students gravely. 'I'm afraid our work here at Deveraux is more important than any single individual. I'm sorry.'

'Say it louder and Cally might hear you,' muttered Jake. 'Welcome to the expendables.'

Ben gripped his shoulder. 'You knew the score when we signed up, Daly. We all did. Cally included.'

'Yeah? Is that supposed to make me feel better? Thought you'd be a tad more concerned, Stanton. How are we gonna win the Sherlock Shield with five?'

'Hey, this isn't about—'

'Ben. Jake.' Now Grant was stern, commanding. 'Bickering has no place in a team. You won't help Cally like that.'

Jennifer laughed humourlessly. 'According to you, we won't help Cal anyway.'

'The thing is,' Lori put in, 'we know exactly where Nemesis is now. This is our chance to destroy it. That's Spy High work, isn't it, Mr Grant? And if we can rescue Cally at the same time . . .'

Grant acknowledged Lori's point. 'Good in principle, Lori. But in practice? We don't yet have a way of attacking Nemesis, though our scientists are working on it, obviously. If only Professor Newbolt was able to contribute. Without him, our chances are slim.'

Newbolt, Lori was thinking. If they only had old Gadge. Well, and hope fluttered in her heart, perhaps they did.

Eddie remained in the virtual reality chamber long after the others had departed. They hadn't called for him to follow them. They hadn't registered his absence. And why should they, he thought bitterly, he was nothing.

Cally lay there, a ghost beneath the glass. He gazed at her. She was like a photograph. 'There's no one I'd sooner have at my back', she'd said. Maybe she ought to think again. If she could think at all.

'I'm sorry, Cal.' Not very witty. Not very joker in the pack.

Eddie saw his face reflected in the cyber-cradle's shield. The spy with a smile. Not any more.

What she was going to do, was it ethical? Was it right? Did the ends justify the means? Lori wasn't sure. All she knew was that one person and one person alone held the possibility of saving Cally. It wasn't her. In a way, it wasn't even Gadge. The one person was Vanessa.

She found Gadge in his lab, fussing over circuit boards and flashing lights, mumbling advice to non-existent students. He didn't even notice her come in. Happy in his own way, Lori thought, senility insulating him from pain and hurt and the memories that scar. And she was here to remind him of all that tragedy. She was here to raise the dead.

'Grandfather,' she said. 'Grandfather.'

Gadge shuddered, looked up. There was a sudden fear in his face, like the discovery of a guilty secret. 'Who is it?' he said. 'Who's there?'

'You know who I am, Grandfather.' She stepped closer towards him, bringing back the past. She smiled.

And old Gadge smiled, too, and relief and delight were mixed together in that smile. It lit up his whole face as he held out his frail arms to embrace her. 'Vanessa,' he said, in a voice choked with emotion. 'My dear.'

Lori let him hug her. She heard the old man sob. She knew why. 'It's good to see you again, Grandfather,' she said.

'Let me look at you, Vanessa.' His gnarled and quivering hands roamed over her face, her hair, the way a blind man might identify someone he knows. 'Ah, you visit me so rarely these days, my dear. You don't know how much I miss you.'

'I do, Grandfather, but you mustn't. There's no need. I'm happy where I am.' Lori thought she'd better move matters along quickly. The deception was troubling her more the longer it lasted. Think of Cally, she reminded herself. This is for Cally.

Gadge seemed to age visibly. 'Happy? How can you be, Vanessa? I did something, didn't I? I did something to make you go away and I was wrong, it was my fault, wasn't it? I can't quite remember what I did but if you stay a while I'm sure I will . . .'

'It doesn't matter, Grandfather,' Lori soothed. 'Not any more. That's what I came to say. It doesn't matter what you did. I forgive you. I've always loved you and I forgive you.'

'You forgive me, Vanessa?' Old Gadge held back the tears with difficulty. 'Oh, my dear, how I hoped you'd one day tell me that. I'm sorry for what I did, so terribly sorry. But I thought . . . I can't remember what I thought . . . but thank you, my dear. I've always loved you, too.' He held her hand and stroked it like it was a kitten.

'Grandfather.' Now was the moment of truth. 'There's something else.'

'Anything for you, Vanessa. Anything, my dear girl.'

'I need you to help me.'

Jennifer opened the door to him, but while Jake didn't expect her to fling her arms around him, certainly not given the present circumstances, he didn't expect the coldness and the sternness in her expression, either. It was as if the more important door, the one that provided access to Jennifer's heart and soul, was not only closed but had been fitted with new chains.

'Lori's not here,' Jennifer said, and smiled thinly like she'd made a joke.

'What?'

'You can come in and have a look if you don't believe me. Bathroom, wherever. She's not even under the bed.'

'What?' Jake wondered about going out and coming in again. 'I'm not looking for Lori, Jen, I don't understand why . . .' He never thought of Simon Macey. 'I came to see you.'

'So you've seen me. I hope it's made you happy.' She gave him a quick twirl.

'Are you all right, Jen?' He was thinking about what Ben had said – *unstable*. 'I thought maybe we could talk. You know, maybe it'd help us if we talked.'

'Talked about what? The nice weather we're having for the time of year? Who you might happen to meet in the grounds when taking a walk?'

'About Cally, actually.'

'Oh, Cally. She's in a coma, did you know that? Still, means we can do things behind her back and she won't be any the wiser. Kind of useful when you think about it, isn't it?'

'Listen, I know we're all upset, but . . .' Jake didn't know quite how to take Jennifer's behaviour. He was beginning to wish Lori *was* there. Or, indeed, anyone. 'And I thought we could talk about us, maybe.'

'*Us?*' Jennifer seemed incredulous. 'Us as in you and me? Just the two of us?'

'Well, the other day, in the dome, in the field, I thought something was maybe happening. You know, between us. I thought we were beginning to feel . . .'

'What?' Why was he saying this after she'd seen him with Lori?

'Listen, Jen, why don't we sit down and talk?'

'I don't think so, Jake.' He'd betrayed her. She couldn't rely on him. She couldn't rely on anyone. 'I'm otherwise occupied. But I'm sure you'll find someone who's interested. If you know what I mean.'

Jake didn't, but he left anyway. He couldn't deal with Jennifer in this mood. If she wanted to be alone, then she was going the right way about it.

He headed back to his own room. Maybe someone had come up with a plan for helping Cally. Anything would do, however unlikely or outrageous, just so long as it was action. He'd never felt comfortable talking. Fighting, though, that was another matter.

Lori found Ben in the virtual reality chamber. He was with Cally, head bowed, deep in thought. His hand rested on the cyber-cradle. He only realised Lori was there when hers joined his and squeezed reassuringly.

'You've got to watch that,' Lori chided gently. 'Not good for a secret agent to get crept up on so easily.'

Ben smiled weakly. 'I wish I could say I knew it was you, Lo. Maybe I'm just getting slack.'

'No,' comforted Lori. 'What's happened to Cally's just affecting us all. But listen, Ben —'

'Do you think I'm a good leader, Lori?'

She was startled by the question, but could tell from Ben's frank expression that it was intended seriously.

'It's something Jake said. He made out that the only reason I was concerned about Cally was because of the impact her loss might have on the team. Like I didn't really care about her at all.'

'Jake didn't mean it,' Lori said. 'He was lashing out without thinking, that's all. We all say things when we're stressed that we don't really mean.'

'You don't, Lo,' Ben said. 'You never lose your temper. You're never sarcastic. You never do things behind people's backs.'

'Oh, Ben,' Lori coloured and shook her head. 'Don't believe it. I'm not a saint.'

'You're an Angel,' Ben smiled. 'But me, I sometimes think I'm down there in the other place with the guys with the horns and the forked tails. Because whatever you say, and however right you might be about Jake and what he said, I'm afraid part of it might be true.'

'Ben, you're tormenting yourself for no reason.'

'No, I've got a reason. It's called selfishness. It's called arrogance. It's called wanting to be the best at any cost. And it makes me act sometimes in ways that I reckon a good leader shouldn't act, and it makes me treat people sometimes, I don't know, like they're less than me.'

'You're strong, Ben. You push us. You make Bond Team what we are.'

'Did I make Cally what she is now?'

'Of course not.' Lori shook him, angered now. 'Nobody's to blame for Cally. None of us. You were right what you said before. We all knew the risks. If we can't take them then we can be mind-wiped and sent home. Blaming ourselves for something that's not our fault, that's self-pity and self-indulgence. That's the sign of a bad leader. A good leader accepts what's done and tries to put it right.'

Ben indicated Cally's cyber-cradle. 'So how do we put this right?'

Lori gripped his hand more tightly. 'That's what I wanted to tell you.'

There were others in the lab, too, the rest of Bond Team, and Grant, even Deveraux via a videscreen link, but Professor Henry Newbolt seemed to be largely unaware of them. Gadge only had eyes for Lori, and they were eyes that once again blazed with genius and originality. For the moment, at least, the inventor was back.

'This is how we'll do it, my dear,' he explained. 'This is how we'll save your friend.'

Eddie expected Gadge to produce a variation on a ray-gun or something, a weapon that would blast Nemesis into a million spidery pieces. Instead, the scientist produced a garment in shimmering silver material, not unlike a one-piece ShockSuit. It reminded him of the old radiation suits they'd used to wear at atomic plants, not one inch of skin exposed, a filmy visor shielding the face. The old Eddie, the spy with a smile, would have made a quip about the lack of fashion sense being enough to frighten Nemesis away, or that he hadn't realised that Gucci was outfitting Spy High students now, or something equally inane. The new Eddie, the Eddie who was nothing, watched closely and listened attentively. If there was a second chance coming, he wasn't going to miss it.

'You need to go back into the program,' Gadge was continuing. 'That's the only way. But you need to make yourselves immune to the power of the virus. Hence the VIPR. The Virus Protection Suit. Set a snake to snare a spider, Vanessa.'

'Vanessa?' Everybody but Ben turned to Lori quizzically.

Lori ignored them all. 'Go on, Grandfather.' More general bemusement. 'What exactly does the suit do?'

'When activated,' Gadge supplied, 'the VIPR generates a force-field that acts as a counteragent to the virus's ability to influence and reprogram cyber-space. In other words, with your suits switched on Nemesis won't be able to harm you. You'll wear these in your cyber-cradles to protect your bodies while virtual versions will be configured into the software so that you'll also be safe in the program itself.'

'Sounds good,' Jake approved.

'If it works,' Jennifer sulked.

'Oh, it'll work.' Gadge seemed inordinately positive. 'I wouldn't create anything for my Vanessa that didn't . . . work . . .' Suddenly a shadow crossed his smile.

Lori interpreted it as bad news. 'How, Grandfather?' Keep his mind off the past. Make Gadge believe in the present. 'How does it work?'

'Oh, in simple terms,' the old man rallied, 'the VIPR resembles the way the human immune system produces anti-bodies to fight infection, only instead of anti-bodies, the suit generates anti-binaries, computer code that defends against even super-viruses such as Nemesis. And better yet, the anti-binaries can attack as well as defend.' Gadge drew his audience's attention to the wrist-bands woven into the suit. 'Functions just like sleepshot, only firing anti-binaries. And for when you've saved . . .' Again, that moment of doubt, of forgetfulness, lucidity ebbing away. 'When . . . you've saved . . . Vanessa?'

'It's all right, Grandfather.' Lori was losing him. The old man's mind was slipping. 'Tell me, what's that? What have you got there?'

Gadge regarded the laptop-sized metal device on the table as if he'd never seen it before. 'What . . . here? A bomb!' It was as if he'd remembered the final answer in a quiz. 'A binary . . . bomb. Set it up . . . set it off . . . Anti-binaries will flood the program . . . break it down entirely. No escape for Nemesis, for anybody caught in the program then. You have to be back before detonation or . . . you can't be saved. No, you can't.' An awful truth at last overwhelmed him. 'Vanessa, I didn't save you . . .' He gazed in tragic horror at Lori. 'I never saved . . .' And then the old eyes glazed, as if the life had left them.

'You're not Vanessa. Who are you? Who are you people? What are you doing in my lab? Can't a man get on with his work without interruption? Leave me alone. Go away and leave me alone . . .' The broken old man who'd once been among the most brilliant minds in the world scuttled muttering into a corner and busied himself with loose strands of wire.

'So are you going to explain what just happened there, Lori?' Jake inquired.

Lori looked after Gadge with pity. 'Something I'm not particularly proud of.'

'But very resourceful of you, Angel.' Deveraux's voice over the videscreen surprised them. 'Using Professor Newbolt's memories of his grand-daughter to effect even a temporary mental recovery. By so doing you have given us a chance, both to save Cross and destroy Nemesis once and for all.'

'But the suits, sir,' Grant cautioned, 'they're untested.'

'We don't have time to test them, Grant,' Deveraux said. 'Time is our enemy. We have to act now, before Nemesis moves on and we lose it. Assemble a team at the virtual reality chamber.'

'Sir!' Ben stepped forward. 'Send us, sir. We know Nemesis better than anyone here, and Cally's one of us. We owe it to her.'

Deveraux's finely chiselled features considered. 'Grant?'

'Stanton has a point, sir, but there are graduate teams—'

'As students, we cannot require you to undertake this mission,' Deveraux pointed out, 'but if it is your wish as a team to volunteer, then you will be assigned. It is your choice, Bond Team. Does Stanton speak for you all?'

It seemed he did. Ben eased into his cyber-cradle as the techs busily prepared the chamber for transfer. Nobody had objected to the mission; everyone had supported him. It had made him feel good, like a leader again, and that was enough. Whatever dangers awaited them when they confronted Nemesis this final time, Ben knew that he and his team-mates would face and overcome them. They were Bond Team. They didn't know how to lose.

'We'll send in a VIPR suit for Cally with you, and the binary bomb. Prime it before you do anything else. Destroying Nemesis is your over-riding priority.'

Lori knew it. She'd deluded Professor Newbolt for this, for the chance to strike back, to stop the virus before it could kill anyone else. Before it could kill Cally. As she strapped herself into her cyber-cradle, Lori hoped that poor, dead Vanessa would have understood. And she prayed that they weren't already too late.

'We're going to be redirecting energy from our security program to the VR systems to ensure that we can transfer you back, but we can't keep that up forever. You'll have an hour. You'll need to locate and rescue Cally within sixty minutes.'

Time limits never bothered Jake. They provided a challenge, not an obstacle. He relaxed his muscles and breathed deeply, as they'd been taught to do before a total virtual reality transfer. He didn't think of Jennifer (though part of him wanted to). He thought of Cally. Last term he'd persuaded her to stay at Spy High. He hadn't done that to see her turned into a vegetable. So they had an hour to put things right. Jake intended to make it count.

'Nemesis has the advantage. It will have been able to rework the program into whatever kind of environment it likes by now. There's no way of knowing what you'll face.'

Jennifer didn't care. The darker, deadlier, more horrific the scenario the better, she was thinking. It would match her mood. The virtual sensors pressed against her temples. She felt the cyber-cradle cramping her, restricting her. She wanted to scream. She wanted to hit out. Soon now. Very soon.

With the slightest of hisses the glass shields of the cyber-cradles descended, clicked into place. 'Good luck, Bond Team,' someone said. The transference began.

Eddie closed his eyes. No more jokes now about two in a cyber-cradle or if they're cradles, why don't they rock, or what happened to the lullabies, or anything like that. The others hadn't encountered Nemesis in the cyber-flesh before. He had, and then he'd been found wanting, but not this time. This time, Eddie vowed, it was going to be different.

SIX

'This is not good,' said Ben.

It was after the apocalypse. All around them were
the smoking skeletons of a ruined city: ruptured roads
and the shells of cars, walls jagged against the sky like
giant and broken teeth, the bones of buildings rotting in
a radioactive wasteland. Above them, clouds were blocking out the pitiful sun. Clouds that were seething and
suppurating like evil itself, stabbing themselves with
scarlet lightning.

'Mankind's final nightmare,' breathed Lori. 'Nuclear
armageddon.'

'Yeah.' Jake's expression was grim behind his visor.
'And Nemesis' ultimate dream. This is what it wants to
see in the real world.'

'Not if we can help it.' Ben adjusted his suit. 'Check
your VIPRS. Make sure they're fully activated. Helmet
communicators all right? Can everybody hear me?'

'Loud and clear, leader man,' said Eddie.

'Good. 'Cause if your suit fails, Nemesis has got you.'

Jennifer stood at a little distance from the others. She was finding the devastated landscape both disturbing and strangely stimulating. 'Well are we doing anything or what?' she demanded restlessly. 'An hour doesn't last forever.'

'We've got to wait, Jen,' Ben reminded her. 'For Cally's suit, and the bomb.'

Alongside Eddie the ground rippled, like it had suddenly become liquid. Solid objects materialised. 'Express delivery,' Eddie said.

'Okay.' Ben knelt by the bomb. 'Lori, stay with me and check I'm doing this right. The rest of you, quick reconnaissance. Any sign of Cally or Nemesis, any sign of anything and I want to know about it.'

Ben focused on priming the bomb. Lori took charge of Cally's bundled suit and watched him proudly. This was the Ben she loved. Decisive. Inspiring. A leader. How could she have been tempted by the sham that was Simon Macey? If they ever got out of here alive, she'd make it up to Ben, she promised.

'So where's the big bad spider, then?' Jennifer wondered, with more than a hint of a sneer.

Eddie and Jake joined her. 'Don't worry,' Eddie said. 'If it's anywhere near, you'll see it. But let me tell you, the longer we can stay out of Nemesis' way, the better.'

'It must know we're here by now,' Jake reasoned. 'Why doesn't it attack?'

'Maybe it doesn't think we're a threat,' Eddie ventured, wondering if more than maybe it was right.

'Jake, Eddie . . .' The sneer had gone from Jennifer's voice. 'What's that?'

Something in the distance, but moving in their direction. Trickling across the cracked and pitted landscape like a thick layer of tar or oil, black, bubbling. A dark tide that washed over everything in its path.

Within minutes, everything in its path would include Bond Team.

'Ben!' Jake called. 'Better make it quick with that bomb. We might be needing it sooner than we thought.'

'All right, we're done,' Ben announced with triumph. 'So what's up?' He and Lori dashed to their team-mates' side.

And the black river was not a single substance after all. They could see that now. It was not a liquid but a swarm of small creatures, glittering like lumps of coal. Like insects. Spiders. A thousand, thousand cyber-spiders scuttling towards them with hostile intent. Nemesis had some new friends.

'It's been breeding. Reproducing itself somehow,' deduced Lori in horror.

'Let's hope Cally's off the other way,' Eddie gulped. ''Cause I think that's where we should be.'

They turned.

They were surrounded.

'Well here's where we check out the suits,' Ben gritted. 'Form a circle. Make a stand. Fry these suckers.'

They didn't need to aim. Their wrist-guns blasted the advancing army with anti-binary particles exactly as Gadge had described, scorching swathes of fire through their numbers. The cyber-bodies crisped and curled like old leaves on a bonfire. The stench of burning rose to further pollute the air.

'Yeah!' Eddie was first to use both wrist weapons at the same time, zig-zagging blazing mayhem with abandon. 'Yeah!' He was beginning to feel a lot better.

Jennifer too was finding release in the slaughter, but Ben was controlling his own urge to indulge in emotional outbursts. A leader had to keep cool even in times of stress. A leader had to consider and assess all conceivable eventualities. And one rather disturbing possibility had just occurred to him.

What if their wrist-bands ran out of power? What if the supply of anti-binaries dried up? And what if Nemesis' brood kept on coming?

They were already only metres away.

'Conserve your power!' Ben yelled. 'We don't know how long the suits can last. Fire one weapon only!'

'You're the boss,' responded Eddie, 'but I reckon we need more firepower, not less.'

A ring of flame protected Bond Team, cindering the cyber-spiders that surged blindly into it. But there were so many of them. Like lemmings, they came on. And suddenly some of them were through and they were launching themselves at the teenagers' bodies. Jake cried out as several of the things impacted on his chest. He jerked instinctively to swipe them away. Didn't need to. The suit, crackling with anti-binaries itself, turned the creatures into flares. They shrivelled. They died. But always, they had replacements.

They leaped at Lori's visor, attacking the eyes. She saw their quivering forms for the slightest of seconds before her sight was dazzled by their bursting into flames. And then, shockingly, heart-stoppingly, they weren't bursting into anything. They weren't even getting sunburn. They were clinging on, clogging her vision. She swept at them with her hand and realised with even greater terror that her wrist-gun was also less effective now, drained of its killing power. 'Ben!' They were crawling all over her. 'My suit!' Her visor was blackened with the things. Soon they'd be gnawing their way through the flimsy material, their fangs at her face. 'Ben!' Lori screamed.

Then they were gone. Ben was holding her and the others were close too and the cyber-spiders were in retreat, leaving behind them only the charred remains of their brethren.

Eddie gasped, nearly doubled up with relief and exhaustion. 'So is that a win for us or what?'

'Why have they gone?' Lori wanted to know. 'They could have had us. My suit was losing power by the second. Much longer and . . .' She shuddered.

'Don't worry, Lo. The suit'll recharge itself,' Ben said. *I hope*, he thought.

'But Lori's right,' mused Jake. 'We were on the point of being overwhelmed. I don't understand why . . .'

'So Nemesis isn't a master tactician,' contributed Jennifer. 'Or it wasn't aware that we were on our last legs. Or maybe that was just the first assault.'

'I think I prefer options one and two,' Eddie said.

'If only.' Jake's eyes narrowed. He sensed further danger. The ground under their feet rumbled. It sounded like a subway train but it wasn't.

Bond Team were scattered like ninepins as the street erupted and Nemesis itself rose up among them.

They were fighting for their lives, Senior Tutor Elmore Grant knew. They were battling to save their friend, perhaps to save countless others whom they'd never even met from the madness of Nemesis. And yet you wouldn't know it, not as their bodies slumbered peacefully in the cyber-cradles, bodies that Grant would be sending home in boxes if the mission went wrong. And it could go wrong, just as easily as it could go right. A Spy High training was no guarantee of survival.

Some agents lived, Grant reasoned. Some agents died. And some former agents were forced to endure an existence somewhere between the two. Like himself. The top half of him was living, was flesh and blood and bone, but his legs were synthetic, had been since his final mission in the field and the explosion that had ended his career. In reality, Senior Tutor Elmore Grant was only half a man.

He ran his hands through his hair. So he had to wait. He had to stay here in the virtual reality chamber and guess at the dangers his students were facing. He could pray for them but he couldn't aid them. He was helpless. And it was a terrible thing for a man like himself to be helpless, to be a bystander. But that was all he was. That was what he'd been reduced to. He had to wait.

Bond Team were fighting for their lives, Senior Tutor Elmore Grant knew. How he envied them.

They froze and stared. It was understandable. The sudden appearance of a twelve foot high sentient computer virus in the approximate form of a spider would probably have been sufficient to leave anybody frozen and staring. Unfortunately, Bond Team were not supposed to be just anybody. They were supposed to have been trained to expect the unexpected, to let nothing faze them or delay their purpose. Because for Bond Team, delay could mean death. And it could be instant.

Lori only had time for an impression of Nemesis' massiveness, the crackling of dark energies at its eyes and abdomen and along the razor edges of its eight black legs. Its head swivelled, calculating its enemies' strength. She didn't have time for evasive action. She didn't have time to move at all.

Nemesis lashed at her with one of its legs. The limb caught her and lifted her into the air. She crashed to the fractured street and expected to be dead. The cyber-flesh had glittered like a blade. She should have been sliced open. But she wasn't. Her suit had not been compromised. She was alive.

And if she was alive, she could fight.

Lori scrambled to her feet. The others were already firing their wrist-guns at Nemesis, though still beating a strategic retreat towards her. Flames ignited against the virus' steel sides but none were slowing it down, none were taking hold. Lori sensed renewed power in her suit. Ben had been right. The anti-binaries had recharged themselves. Now it was her turn.

Lori aimed her anger at Nemesis. She fired. Flames exploded at its abdomen.

'Good shooting, Lo!' shouted Ben. 'Are you all right?'

'I'd be better if we could stop this thing in its tracks.'

'We're hurting it!' Jake claimed, and the screeches issuing from Nemesis certainly supported his contention. 'But not enough. We're right in the source of its power here. We're just not packing enough punch.'

'What will it take for this monster to fall?' Jennifer cried.

Then she was ducking, rolling out of the way as the spider's front legs scythed once more through the poisoned air. Bond Team scattered, regrouped, fired again.

Which was a pattern they could probably maintain throughout the remaining minutes of their hour. Which meant it wasn't going to get them anywhere, Ben reasoned. An endless stand-off with Nemesis was not going to locate Cally. They – he – needed to be more proactive.

He hoped to God the VIPRS were everything Gadge had said.

'Ben!' Lori screamed. 'Wait!' Why was he running directly towards the virus?

'Come on, you ugly sucker! Come and get me! Show me what you've got!' And then I'll show you what I've got, Ben promised.

'He's lost it!' Eddie was flabbergasted. 'His mind's gone!'

'Then let's get after him. Why are we even talking?' Jennifer continued her attack.

'No, wait, Jen!' Jake restrained her. 'Ben knows what he's doing.'

But even Nemesis seemed shocked that one of the intruders should offer himself up to his inevitable fate so generously. The organic form was standing within striking distance of its electrodes, shouting defiance and shaking its fists but not even firing the weapons that stung. Such reckless behaviour did not compute with the data Nemesis had gathered on the human species. Such futile demonstrations of bravado were not logical. They deserved to be punished.

Nemesis's head dropped like the guillotine. It swallowed Ben to the waist.

Everyone but Jake cried out in horror. 'Get ready!' Jake urged.

As Nemesis' head exploded.

Sections of skull and brain and eyeball sprayed across the street, fizzling like burned-out circuits. What was left of the cyber-spider's mouth retreated twitching from Ben, who fired his wrist-guns again, disintegrating the head further. His suit was slick with a blood like oil, but he was unharmed.

'Finish it off!' Jake ordered. 'Now!'

The rest of Bond Team charged at the tottering Nemesis, firing furiously. The virus seemed unable to sustain its chosen form now. The brittle legs snapped. The armoured abdomen ruptured and liquid spilled out. The cleansing fires of the anti-binary particles went to work on the creature's grotesque body.

And Nemesis fell in flames to the ground.

'We've done it!' whooped Jennifer. 'We killed you. We *killed* you!'

Lori rushed to Ben's side. He was wobbling. She caught him and eased him down onto one knee. 'Ben,' and she wanted to kiss him but a pair of visors between them was a bit of a problem. 'What on earth? You could have been killed. What did you think you were doing?'

'That was disgusting,' said Eddie, with an expression to match.

'It was the bravest thing I've ever seen.' Lori glared at him.

'Yeah, well,' Eddie adapted, 'that's what I meant, Lo. The bravest most disgusting thing I've ever seen.' And in his head he was thinking: That's why Ben is leader and I'm just the nobody who makes smart remarks. And in his head he was asking: Could I do that? Could I risk sacrificing myself for the others, for the team? And if not, why am I even here? When will my chance come?

'Now that's what I call point-blank range.' Jake nodded his admiration. 'Nice work, Ben.'

'Thanks. Yeah.' Ben's suit was gradually sizzling away all trace of Nemesis' innards. He was pleased about that, even more about his plan's success. 'I reckoned the only way we might be able to overcome Nemesis was if we could get close enough to blast through its defences.'

'Yeah, and you can't get much closer than inside the thing's mouth,' Jake chuckled. 'You've always been a tough act to swallow, Ben.'

'Well, just don't ask me for a repeat performance,' Ben said.

'Nobody's going to need to,' said Lori.

'Uh, guys.' It was Jennifer. She sounded anxious. 'I wouldn't bet on that if I were you. Something's happening. Something not good.'

Nemesis lived. At least, its constituent parts still seemed to be alive. How else could their independent movement be explained, the disturbing ability of loose scraps of casing to inch towards each other and fuse themselves together, circuit seeking circuit, shards of limbs combining and extending?

'It's reconstructing itself,' Jennifer observed with awe. 'It's a cyber-resurrection.'

'So let's kill it again before it screws its head back on.' Eddie looked like he wanted to lead the way.

Ben struggled to his feet, leaning on Lori. He shook his head despondently. 'It's no good, Eddie. It didn't work, after all. We can't kill it, whatever we do, not completely, not with anything less than the bomb.'

'So what do we do, Ben?' Jennifer watched as legs snapped together like poles, as the creature's abdomen inflated like a balloon. 'It's getting the hang of this.'

'W'

'we've no choice,' Ben decided. 'We leave Nemesis to the bomb. We can't kill it but it can't kill us either, not in the VIPRS. So we find Cally. Right now.'

They moved off quickly across the decimated landscape, though Jennifer couldn't resist a final, parting gesture. A clump of eyeballs squirmed its way past her foot to join the rest of Nemesis' head. One brief blast of her wrist-gun and it was bonfired. 'Fix that,' she muttered.

They spread out in a line to cover the maximum ground possible, picking their way across the crumbling city and keeping in constant touch with each other through their helmet communicators. On missions, it was good to talk, even if most of the time it had to be in whispers or monosyllables or both.

'Watch where you tread,' hissed Ben, proving the point. 'Lots of holes and stuff. You fall down one of those and it's bad news. Your suits can't mend a broken leg.'

Eddie wondered whether that meant that if any of them did suffer an accident here among the ruins, Ben would lead their team-mates on regardless. He doubted it, but he was feeling pretty left behind as it was, relegated to the far end of the line. He shouldn't take it personally, he knew. After all, there was another end of the line with Jennifer on it, but somehow he just felt distanced from the heart of things. Maybe if he could spot Cally, then everything would be all right.

But even that privilege was denied him.

'Ben! All of you!' Jennifer was not whispering now. 'Over here! Over here!'

Of course, it would be that Eddie had the furthest to go.

'What is it, Jen?' Ben's voice. 'Is it Cally?'

Dismay, almost palpable even over the communicator. 'I think so.'

She thought so? Eddie scrambled desperately over the stone ribs of dead buildings. She thought so? What could Jennifer see? What horrors had he abandoned Cally to?

He heard his team-mates, one by one as they reached Jennifer's position. 'Oh, my God . . . I don't believe it . . . Ben . . .'

They were just up ahead now, crouched low and peering over a ridge of rubble. At Cally? He raced to their side. 'What is it? What is it?'

'Eddie, keep down!' Ben ordered.

Eddie dropped to the ground. He saw Ben and Jake ashen-faced, the girls horrified, disgusted. He lifted his head to see what they had seen.

And then he knew why.

SEVEN

In what once had been a doorway, in what once had been a wall, Cally was hanging. One arm was above her, almost like it was waving, while the other dangled at her side. Her legs were crooked, like a broken doll's, and neither reached the ground. They didn't have to. Cally was held in place by a web that had been strung between the doorposts, a web in which she was hopelessly enmeshed, a web that might have been the work of a spider but for the current that seemed to hum through it and that made its strands more like electric wires or cables.

Worse, the ground around Cally was thick with cyber-spiders, swarming at the base of the web, crawling over the shattered bricks, even daring to climb Cally's unflinching legs, speckling her skin like the march of some foul disease.

And worse still, Nemesis itself, towered above Cally. Unmarked. Unwounded. Reborn. The calculations behind its rows of restored eyes seeming to say one thing: bait.

But worst of all was Cally's possible condition. Her head was lolling drunkenly.

'She's not moving.' Lori said what the others were thinking. 'Ben, what if we're too late? What if Cally's . . . you know . . .'

'We're not. She's not.' Ben defied reality to disagree. 'She's just unconscious. We just have to get her off that web, get the suit on her, and all go home. Then this place gets blown to bits.'

'And soon,' Jennifer reminded him. 'So how do we get rid of Nemesis?'

Ben considered quickly. 'We need a diversion. If we split into two groups, me and Lori, you, Jen, Jake and . . . Eddie?'

No sign of him.

'Where'd he go?'

'I didn't notice. He was just here . . .'

'If he's playing some kind of stupid game . . .' warned Ben.

'I don't think so,' judged Jake. 'I think you've got yourself your diversion. Look.'

This was his chance. As soon as he saw Cally caught in Nemesis' webbing like that, those loathsome bugs all over her, he knew it. This was the moment for Eddie Nelligan to prove himself, to redeem himself. And he wasn't going to blow it.

He slipped away with frightening ease while the others were still staring at Cally and Nemesis. He could be decisive when he wanted to be. He was thinking diversion before Ben had even introduced the word, and it seemed clear to him the only kind of diversion that could work. Eddie circled away from the others. It wasn't going to be good enough for him or anyone else simply to distract Nemesis' attention. The virus knew that in their VIPRS they couldn't be hurt. If the suit was deactivated, however, Nemesis might be persuaded to clear a space next to Cally.

Eddie broke cover, edged out into the decimated area where Cally was being held. It might have been the uneven surface of the rubble that was making his legs shake or it might not. Any moment now and Nemesis could be on him.

'Eddie, what do you think you're doing? Get down, Eddie. It'll see you . . . Can you hear me, Eddie? Take cover. That's an order . . .'

But now was not the time for Eddie to listen to orders. 'Calm down, Ben,' he said, far from calm himself, 'or you'll do yourself an injury. I'm going to lead Nemesis away, and when I do, go in for Cal. See you later.' The eternal optimist. The spy with a smile.

'Eddie, this is not . . .'

He deactivated his communicator. He deactivated his suit.

Nemesis sensed him immediately. It raised its head like an animal sniffing a new smell. Something had changed in the virtual world, and it seemed to the virus' advantage.

Eddie gave it some help. 'Hey, ugly, I'm from Rent-a-Victim. Seems you've been in touch with an . . .' He didn't finish the sentence. The force of Nemesis' hate slammed into him like a Light Train at full speed. Eddie fell to his knees, clasping his ears, not even able to hear himself screaming. No protection. No active anti-binaries to insulate him from the psychic assault.

Through vision blistered with pain he saw the virus stalking towards him. If he didn't get up, if he didn't get moving, that Rent-a-Victim quip could be his epitaph.

Eddie staggered to his feet, turned and ran, wishing he had a SkyBike handy. He didn't look behind. It wouldn't be encouraging to watch Nemesis gaining on him like an eight-legged Angel of Death. Besides, he had to concentrate on the terrain, the treacherously loose piles of rubble, the sudden gaping pits and slants of fallen wall. If he fell, there'd be no getting up again.

He hoped the others would be with Cally now. He'd given them their opening.

Eddie darted through a doorway where Nemesis could not follow, and this building's surviving wall was big. The virus would have to go round. It'd slow it down.

Only it didn't. Nemesis smashed through the wall and kept on coming.

Maybe this hadn't been such a good idea, after all. But surely he'd lured the creature far enough away? Surely he could afford to reactivate his suit?

The ground subsided in front of him. Eddie cried out, tipped forward, felt the world collapsing, a singing in his ears, and the sickening thud of impact.

Eddie groaned. He'd plunged into some sort of cellar, landed on his back. He tried to move. His legs were trapped beneath a slab of concrete. At least they didn't feel broken. And at least his arms were free. All he had to do was reactivate his suit and either wait for the others or wait for the transfer. It could only be minutes now.

All he had to do was reactivate his suit . . .

All he had to do was . . .

All . . . over.

The suit must have been damaged in the fall. Nothing was happening.

'Eddie, this is not the way. Get back . . . He's turned off his communicator.' Ben gaped at the others, as if Eddie's temerity at cutting him off in mid-command was the most shocking thing of all.

'Nemesis has seen him,' Jennifer observed. 'It's after him!'

'He's either more stupid or more courageous than we've ever given him credit for,' said Jake.

'We've got to help him!' declared Lori, already on her feet.

Ben caught hold of her arm, gently but firmly. 'No. Eddie's made his choice. Our priority's Cally. Let's get down there before Nemesis calls off the chase.'

There was no advantage in concealing themselves further. With a whoop of battle the remaining four members of Bond Team launched themselves from the ridge and hurtled towards the captive form of Cally. Their wrist-guns blazed. Half of the cyber-spiders had ignited before their computer brains even registered the attack. The others scurried to meet the enemy.

'Protect Lori!' Ben ordered. 'She's got Cally's suit. Keep her between us!'

He took the lead himself, Lori dropping behind him

and Jennifer and Jake on the flanks. Well-aimed anti-binaries scorched a clear path to the doorway. Cyber-spiders threw themselves from atop the wall; Bond Team's accuracy turned them into tiny fireballs.

Ben sliced through the webbing. Lori caught Cally as she fell, lowered her as gently as possible to the ground. She knelt by her friend's side anxiously, smoothed the hair away from her face, called her name and prayed she was alive. But Cally seemed cold and inanimate. It didn't look good.

'How is she, Lori?' Ben and the others encircled them, keeping the diminishing number of cyber-spiders at bay.

'I don't know. I don't know.' Lori rubbed Cally's limp hands, cradled her close. 'Cally, can you hear me? Cally? I can't get a response, Ben. I don't know what to do!'

'Get the suit on her,' prompted Jake.

Awkwardly, clumsily, Lori unrolled Cally's VIPRS and thrust her limbs into it. It was like dressing an unwieldy and oversized baby. 'Come on. Cally,' she was murmuring. 'Come on. Come on. Speak to me. Say something.' But even with the suit on, there was silence. 'Jake, it isn't . . .'

And then a cough, a splutter, a fragile twitch of the head and flutter of the eyelids.

'Cally! Guys, she's alive!' Lori hugged her friend ardently. 'Cally, you're all right. It's going to be all right.'

'Looking that way,' Jake said. He ceased firing. Ben and Jennifer followed suit. The ground around them was black with charred and smoking bodies. None were left to trouble them.

'Yeah, well let's not start counting chickens,' Ben cautioned, 'or even spiders. Not until we've put the whole of cyber-space between us and Nemesis.' He consulted the chronometer in his suit. 'And that should be in about three minutes.'

Jake grinned. 'Which just gives us time to welcome Sleeping Beauty here back into the land of the living. Hey, Cal, how are you?'

She was weak and disorientated, but nothing worse than that, it seemed. The medics would be able to check her out properly when they got back, Ben knew. He didn't kneel alongside her with the others. Rather, he turned away and gazed out across the ravaged city. Ben doubted it was appropriate for a leader to show emotion.

'What's . . . happened?' Cally gripped Lori's hand in alarm. 'Where are we?'

'It doesn't matter. Just relax, Cal,' Lori counselled. 'Everything's fine.'

But Cally didn't seem convinced. Her eyes flitted between her team-mates. 'Eddie,' she said. 'I remember . . . Eddie was here. Where is he? Where's Eddie?'

Bond Team glanced at each other guiltily. It was a good question.

Maybe he'd be all right anyway. Maybe Nemesis would lose track and just pass him by. Maybe he wouldn't need to do anything but lie quietly where he was and bide his time until the transfer sequence . . .

Yep, and maybe there were pigs up there in the torn and tumultuous sky.

Eddie shoved again at the concrete slab on his legs.

Arnold Schwarzenegger III probably bench-pressed weights like this before breakfast without even raising a sweat, but working out had never worked out for Eddie Nelligan. And it was too late to start now.

If Nemesis appeared before the transfer, he was dead meat.

But strangely, somehow, Eddie didn't feel like screaming or bursting into tears or breaking into prayer. If anything, he felt satisfied, contented. He'd proved himself at last, to the others, and to himself. They'd have rescued Cally by now. He trusted them to have done that. His sacrifice, if sacrifice it was doomed to be, was not going to be in vain.

And maybe he'd be all right anyway.

Only he wouldn't. A shadow closed over the cellar like an eclipse. A black shape loomed. Nemesis peered down at him and its evil glee raked at Eddie's mind like talons. He wouldn't cry out. He wouldn't give Nemesis the pleasure.

How long before the transfer? Seconds, surely. If he could just delay the virus, play for time.

'Wait! Don't! Listen to me! I can help you!'

Nemesis wasn't falling for it. A leg like a titanic javelin quivered in mid-air, selecting its spot with sadistic precision.

Last time, Eddie had been dismissed as a worthless irritation. This time, no such luck.

When it jabbed down, the creature's leg would pierce him just above the navel and plunge right through his body to burst out of his back. He'd be wriggling like an insect on a pin.

Transfer. *Transfer!*

Eddie couldn't help it. He had to scream.

He felt a tingling in his bones.

Certain death speared towards him.

Someone up there loved Eddie Nelligan. Must do.
Because instead of Nemesis running him through in one
fatal motion, helpful pairs of human hands were on him
and hauling him hastily from the cyber-cradle. His
scream reinterpreted itself as a hoot of laughter. The
transfer had performed the nick of time routine. He was
back in the virtual reality chamber. Spy with a smile? He
was spy in one piece, and that was good enough.

But what about the others? What about Cally?

'Eddie! You're all right!' Lori was already approaching him, attended by her own cluster of concerned techs.
She seemed glad to see him. Genuinely. Proved it by
flinging her arms around him and hugging him tightly. If
he'd got his visor up more quickly he might have got a
kiss out of her as well. 'We were so worried. You were so
brave.'

'Yeah, well, some of us are just gifted that way,' Eddie
said modestly. He noticed medics rushing into the
chamber, bringing with them oxygen and a stretcher.
'Cally?'

'She's weak but she's going to be fine,' said Lori.
'Come on.'

She did look weak as the medics lifted her out of her
cyber-cradle and on to the stretcher. Ben, Jake and
Jennifer looked on anxiously. 'Way to go, Ed,' said Jake,
but still only managing a half-smile.

'Eddie?' Cally seemed dazed, scarcely conscious. 'Eddie.' She reached out her hand towards him. Eddie took it and squeezed reassuringly. 'Thank you for coming back.'

'Well, I couldn't just leave you there.' Eddie grinned. 'You owe me a smoothie, Cal.'

Cally smiled drowsily. 'I owe you more than that.'

'Okay, enough for now,' said one of the medics. 'We need to get her checked out in the infirmary. Are we ready?'

Cally was wheeled away. She already seemed to be asleep. But that was all right, sleep was a restorative. And sleep was not coma.

'Eddie.' Ben gripped his arm. 'That stunt you pulled with Nemesis, what were you trying to prove?'

'Ben, I . . .'

'And who cares anyway? Whatever it was, I reckon you proved it.' And he shook Eddie by the hand. Warmly.

Eddie wondered briefly whether he might not still be in virtual reality. Ben Stanton shaking him by the hand? It couldn't be for real, could it? And here were Senior Tutor Grant and Corporal Keene, looking like they were ready to join the congratulations. And the tech's voice reverberating through the chamber from the control room: 'Binary bomb detonated. Impact of anti-binary particles successful. Virtual scenario and everything within it eliminated.' Danger over. Threat removed. World saved. Too good to be true, surely?

Sadly, Eddie was right.

The cyber-cradles started to shake, the mechanisms flashed, sparked as circuits overloaded.

'Are they supposed to do that?' Eddie wondered.

'Get back,' Ben warned. Instinctively, Bond Team moved closer together. 'What's happening?' To the nearest tech: 'Is this something to do with the bomb?'

The hapless tech didn't look like he had any idea.

But the cyber-cradles were rattling now, like something was inside them struggling to be let out, like something huge and powerful was restless to be born. The glass shields exploded. Bolts of searing light lanced to the ceiling, driving everyone further back. A shrill scream of release battered the eardrums.

A sound Bond Team had heard before.

'My God!' Jennifer realised with shock. 'It's Nemesis! It's coming through!'

And it was. Within the pillars of light the air darkened, danced in strange shapes and patterns, thickened into substance, shadowed and solidified.

In the virtual reality chamber, a giant cybernetic spider was materialising.

'It's followed us,' Jake gasped.

Followed him, Eddie thought woefully. Nemesis had been closest to him at the time of transfer. So he hadn't saved the world after all. He'd doomed it.

The stalks of the legs filled in, the bulging abdomen formed, the hideous black head took shape.

'This is impossible,' someone said unhelpfully.

'Turn the power off!' Ben was suddenly shouting. 'All of it. Shut everything down! It's feeding off the power and using it to materialise. Kill the power and kill Nemesis!'

Grant barked the order: 'Power off! Now!'

The tech in the control room heard. Obeyed. The virtual reality chamber was plunged into lifeless darkness. Nemesis screeched again. It was a shadow among shadows now, the cold stuff of nightmares.

'You're dead,' Jennifer gloated.

Yet as it writhed and screamed and seemed to sense its unnatural life ebbing away, hatred drove Nemesis on. The creature glared at its enemies, Lori was certain she saw the evil glitter within its eyes. There was no time to run as Nemesis lunged towards them, its body fusing, crackling, and toppling. A massive, irresistable weight.

Lori cringed instinctively, threw up her hands.

And the falling form of Nemesis shattered against them, brittle and harmless. It was like a phantom, like a fume. Lori shuddered at the impact as if she'd suddenly been shut in a freezer, but the effect was brief. Without the sustenance of electricity, without the nourishment of cyber-space, Nemesis could no longer exist. There was the echo of a final, futile howl, like distant static, like feedback.

Then Nemesis was no more.

'Can we get some lights back in here?' Grant's voice.

Lights flooded the chamber like hope. The cyber-cradles were ruined but they could be rebuilt. The important thing was that Nemesis had been destroyed. Bond Team looked at each other and hardly seemed able to believe it. For a second, silence. Then whoops of glee and an outbreak of hugging and back-slapping. Even Corporal Keene seemed prepared to express solidarity, if a little gruffly.

Lori embraced Jake, who alone among her teammates seemed less than ecstatic, almost grim. She knew why. She squeezed his hands with secret meaning. Nemesis might have been eliminated, yes, but they still had one problem remaining.

It was time to deal with Simon Macey.

EIGHT

'**I**'m really glad you're okay, Lori,' said Simon Macey. 'I was really worried. I don't know what I'd have done if something had happened to you.'

Drop dead, Macey, thought Lori. 'Oh, Simon,' she simpered. 'Do you mean it?'

'Of course I mean it. You know how important you are to me, Lori.'

Another day. Another clandestine rendezvous. Another classroom. But it ought to be on a stage, Lori was thinking. A theatre would be an appropriate setting for a pair of such palpably false performances as these. If the spy game ever fell through, she and Simon both had a future in acting.

Here he was moving towards her, disarming her with That Smile. His hands would be on her next and she'd have to endure them. It was part of the plan. 'In fact,' said Simon, 'when you were endangered by the Nemesis virus, it just made me realise I can't do without you. That's the truth.'

'I believe you, Simon.' Like hell.

The hands. On her shoulders. That Smile leering like a mask inches from her face. She could probably break his nose from here, give him something to really smile about. But keep the anger in, Lori. Play the Angel. Remember your lines.

'And Simon, I feel the same.'

'You do?'

'Being so close to death focused my mind, made me see things clearly. I saw you clearly, Simon, maybe for the first time.' *You oily creep.* 'I know now it's you I want to be with. No, let me finish. I don't think it's fair on the others to let this out before Last Team Standing, but afterwards, I want everyone to know about you and me.'

'Oh, Lori,' said Simon Macey, 'afterwards they will.'

There'd be an embrace now (and there was). She'd have to feel him pressing against her (she did). And his hands like a customs official frisking for drugs. Stroking the back of her neck, beneath her hair. And there was kissing, too, and rather a lot of it (at least she had mouth-wash back in her room).

'Lori,' said Simon Macey, 'you don't know how happy you've made me.'

Lori smiled innocently. 'Simon,' she said, 'the best is yet to come.'

'But he didn't say anything to persuade you to sabotage our efforts in Last Team Standing or to pass on information about tactics or anything like that?' Jake sat thoughtfully on Lori's bed.

'Nothing like that,' Lori called from the bathroom, 'unless I was so keen to get out of there that I missed it.' She emerged wearing her bathrobe and towelling her wet hair. 'I needed a shower. Something to wash off the stink of hypocrisy.'

Jake tried not to notice too much of Lori's bare flesh. 'Well, he's got to be wanting to use you somehow.'

'Ain't that the truth. And very unpleasant it was, too.' Lori wound the towel round her hair like a turban.

'He must have said something. He must have done something.' Jake got up and paced the room. 'Macey wouldn't have missed a golden opportunity like that.'

'Am I making you uncomfortable, Jake? If you want to step outside, it won't take a second to put some clothes on.'

'No, don't bother.' Jake blinked as Lori raised her eyebrows amusedly. 'I mean, we haven't got the time. I know Cally's still in the infirmary, but Jen could be back any minute and she won't want to see me here, that's for sure.'

'No? From what Cally told me about the dome, I thought you two might be on the point of becoming an item. You look good together.'

Jake shrugged. 'Try telling that to Jen. I mean, I like her, Lori, I like her a lot, but just when I think we're getting somewhere some kind of weird alarm bell goes off in Jennifer's head and the shutters come down and it's like I've grown a second head or something. I don't understand her.'

Lori sighed sympathetically. 'Well, we all know that Jen has issues she's got to sort out. I guess if we could trace their source back into her past somehow we could help her come to terms with them, but if I were you, Jake—'

'Wait! Lori.' Jake snapped his fingers.

'What's—?'

'Where did Macey touch you?' Jake inspected Lori's bathrobed body like Sherlock Holmes himself scrutinising for clues. 'Exactly where?'

'Exactly just about everywhere,' said Lori. 'I don't know about license to kill. A license to take liberties, that's Simon. But I'm not sure I'm following you, Jake.'

'It's got to be a part of you that you scarcely even see yourself.'

'I beg your pardon?'

'You said the magic word, Lori,' Jake grinned. 'Trace their source. *That's* how Macey's going to use you in Last Team Standing. He's planted a tracer on you. You'll be giving away our position and you won't even know it.'

'But I'd have noticed . . .'

'Not necessarily.' Jake's sharp eyes narrowed. 'Lean your head forward, like you're nodding off to sleep in one of Grant's History of Espionage lessons. That's it.' He pored over the delicate skin of Lori's exposed neck, pushed the towel up to analyse the very roots of her hair. Jake laughed. 'I knew it. I knew it!'

'What? Blonde's my natural colour.'

'No. Feel. Feel the back of your neck.' He helped to guide Lori's fingers to the black dot smaller than a fingernail that was affixed to skin which would normally be obscured by her hair. 'It is a tracer. I was right. Lori, my dear, you've been bugged.'

'Well get it off me, then,' Lori complained. 'I've got a few ideas where I can stick it on Simon Macey, and all of them are painful.'

'I don't think so.' Jake patted Lori's neck and the tracer. 'This little beauty stays where it is.'

'What? Why? So sleazy Simon can monitor my every movement?'

'Exactly,' Jake schemed darkly. 'Macey thinks he's got you where he wants you, Lo. Let him think it. 'Cause when Last Team Standing starts, he's gonna find it's the other way round.'

'What, no grapes?' Eddie rummaged through Cally's bedside table. 'You can't be a proper hospital patient without grapes. I'm afraid it looks like you're going to have to leave and rejoin Bond Team, Cal.'

'Funny,' grinned Cally, propped up by an unfeasible number of pillows. 'That's pretty much exactly what the medic said on his rounds not half an hour ago.'

'Really?' Lori and Jennifer were perched on either side of Cally's bed while the three boys stood. 'That's great news.'

'Did he actually say you could return to active training, Cally?' Ben was more cautious. He was thinking about the day after tomorrow and Last Team Standing. It wasn't called that for nothing. Last Team Lying in a Hospital Bed wouldn't work.

Cally, though, was emphatic. 'He actually did, Ben. Said it'd be the best thing for me and I agree. There wasn't much physically wrong with me anyway, nothing that a few days rest hasn't cured. It was only my mind that Nemesis was trying to mess with.'

'If only there were a few boys like that,' Lori observed archly.

'I don't think Nemesis was quite sure what to make of me,' Cally said. 'Grant thinks that's why I was kept alive in the VR scenario. Nemesis was probing my mind, trying to work me out.'

'It should have known better,' joked Eddie. 'Nobody can work a woman out.'

Jake and Jennifer exchanged a glance that could have meant anything.

'I think it had given up, anyway,' Cally continued. 'If you hadn't come when you did, guys, my mind would have been mush.'

'What?' Ben said. 'You mean like Eddie's?'

'Oh, that's cruel,' Eddie complained.

'I've got a lot to thank you for, all of you.' Cally squeezed Lori's and Jennifer's arms.

'Bond Team look after their own,' said Ben.

'I feel a pep talk coming on,' mouthed Jake.

'And now that we're all together again, and all declared fit, we'd better start focusing on tactics for Last Team Standing.' Ben never missed a trick, Jake thought, in a kind of grudging admiration. 'I hope I don't need to remind anyone how important this final event is. Palmer and Hannay teams have already been eliminated, so it's us against Macey's lot, and we can only win the Sherlock Shield if we take them in Last Team Standing. We're close, but we're not there yet.'

'Don't worry about it, Ben,' said Jennifer. 'The day we can't beat Solo Team one on one is the day we deserve to get mind-wiped and sent home.'

'I'm glad you're confident, Jen,' Ben approved, 'but don't forget the scores. Because of the Spyscapes debacle—' Lori registered with gratitude that Ben didn't mention the Gun Run — 'Solo Team are ahead. Not by much, maybe, but it gives them an edge. What it boils down to is that we can't afford a single casualty. We have to eliminate every one of Macey's lot without losing a life ourselves. So we need to be sharp, and I mean sharp.'

'Any sharper, leader man,' said Eddie, 'and I'd be cutting myself.'

'Very funny, Eddie.' Ben regarded his team-mates warningly. 'But Macey's going to do whatever he can to win, by fair means or foul, and don't you forget it.'

Lori's eyes met Jake's. They wouldn't.

Grant had introduced the Last Team Standing event as the modern equivalent of the late twentieth century craze for paint guns in the forest. He'd shown them old footage of long-dead executives with fat bellies and boiler suits wheezing from one tree to another and firing paint balls at each other with all the accuracy of blind men in the fog. At night. The purpose of the exercise had apparently been to foster a sense of corporate identity and to team-build. The latter was still part of the thinking behind Last Team Standing, and the showdown between Spy High's two leading teams also took place in the real world, no virtual reality or special effects here, but boiler suits had been exchanged for ShockSuits, and paint guns superceded by stasis rifles. The idea remained to stop the opposing team in its tracks, if not dead, then at least temporarily paralysed. And there was an hour in which to do it.

Bond Team checked their weapons as a series of metal posts rose from the ground behind them to a height of about four metres. Lights flashed along each post's length, signifying that the energy fence that marked out the limits of the game-space was activated. Brushing into that invisible barrier now, either accidentally or for some unfair purpose, would earn the culprit not only a nasty shock but immediate exclusion from the event. The competing teams had only a limited area in which to outwit their opponents. Most of it was heavily wooded.

'Right. Three teams of two,' announced Ben. 'Me and Lori. Jake and Jennifer. Cally and Eddie.' Nobody said otherwise, though Jake couldn't help notice Jennifer scowl sulkily. Whatever he'd done wrong, she still hadn't forgiven him. 'Watch each other's backs. We don't want Macey's bunch to get behind us.'

'It's the kind of sneaky, lowdown trick they'll go in for,' disapproved Eddie.

'We want to get behind them.'

'Great tactics, Ben,' Eddie enthused.

'Each pair keep within sight of the others. We don't want to get separated. And you know the call if anybody sees anything.'

Everybody nodded. 'Communicators would help,' Lori noted.

'Yeah, but no electronic aids allowed,' Ben said, 'of any kind.'

Not even tracers, Lori reflected. She felt the back of her neck gingerly, the tiny device like a blister on her skin. Jake winked at her encouragingly.

'Okay,' Ben finished. 'Solo Team'll be entering the game-space from the other side by now. Let's give 'em something to worry about.'

Bond Team delved into the woodland. Jennifer and Jake took the right, Cally and Eddie the left, while Ben and Lori kept the central position. They moved silently, stealthily, senses sharply alert for the slightest sign of human company. The Sherlock Shield depended on the outcome of the next sixty minutes.

Lori saw the intensity on Ben's face, his total commitment to the cause. She could never tell him about Simon Macey and her, never. And she could never tell him that it didn't matter how they crept and crouched and crawled through the forest, Solo Team were going to be bearing down on them with unerring precision thanks to the little bit of help Simon had slapped to the back of her neck. And even if Jake's plan worked here and now, what was to stop Simon from revealing the whole truth to Ben and ruining her life that way? She saw her boyfriend regarding her with concern. 'Don't worry,' he whispered. She wished.

To the left: 'You all right, Cal?' Eddie looking out for his team-mate. 'We can kind of have a bit of a rest if you need to.'

'I'm not an invalid, Eddie,' Cally retorted, though her limbs already felt heavy, slow.

'No, I didn't mean . . .'

'I know you didn't.' Cally corrected her tone. 'But I'm

doing fine. How could I not? I've got the spy with a smile for my partner.'

And when she smiled at him, Eddie found he didn't care whether they won the Sherlock Shield or not.

To the right: 'Listen, Jen.' Jake not being able to bear the silence between them. 'I know this isn't the time or the place, but afterwards, I mean later, we've really got to talk, sort ourselves out.'

'You're right, Jake,' agreed Jennifer coldly.

'I am?'

'This isn't the time or the place.' Her face was closed against him.

Jake sighed. Well, he'd tried. He hoped his plan for the tracer would be more successful. He judged that it was time.

For no apparent reason, Jake made the call of a bird.

Jennifer ducked as low as if it had been the whistle of a bomb. 'What do you think you're doing?'

'I think I see someone,' Jake hissed, taking cover. 'Over there.' He indicated just about the entire forest, emphasised his belief with a second bird-call.

'What are you talking about?' Jennifer squinted into green distances. 'There's nobody over there. Where exactly?'

But it didn't matter now. Jake's real aim had been achieved. The rest of Bond Team squatted down along-side himself and Jennifer, stasis rifles primed. Jake caught Lori's eye ever so subtly and nodded. While the others craned forward, keen to glimpse the enemy, she lagged behind. Nobody noticed her hand apparently massaging the back of her neck.

'What have you got, Jake?' Ben was demanding.

'Macey and Sonia Dark,' Jake lied. 'I'm sure it was them, at least them.'

'I didn't see anything, Ben.' Jennifer wasn't happy. 'There's nothing.'

Ben peered out into the forest. Certainly looked like nothing, but did he want to take chances? Was a good leader the one who took risks or the one who played the percentages? Jake wasn't usually given to flights of fancy.

'I'm telling you,' he stressed. 'Simon. Sonia. Maybe all of Solo Team. Coming our way.' Another surreptitious glance at Lori. This time it was her turn to nod.

'Well . . .' Ben couldn't afford mistakes.

'Ben, there's nothing there.' Jennifer seemed just as convinced as Jake.

'I saw something, too,' claimed Lori. 'It has to be Solo Team.'

Jennifer snapped round to glare at Lori. Of course she would support Jake, even though for some unfathomable reason they were both clearly lying. But Lori's intervention had convinced Ben.

'Okay, we'll fall back,' he planned. 'We'll form a defensive semi-circle the other side of this piece of open ground. If they haven't seen us, maybe we can pick one or two of them off. Let's do it.'

Bond Team retreated, spaced themselves out and created an arc enclosing the perfect killing ground, if anyone was unwise enough to wander into it. With her tracer now removed and adorning the undergrowth, Lori reasoned, the chances of that were good. Bring 'em on. Bring 'em all on.

They didn't have long to wait. 'What did I tell you?' grinned Jake. He didn't dare look at Lori in case he burst into triumphant laughter.

'I don't believe it,' gaped Jennifer.

But there was no denying it now. Stealing between the trees at the limits of their vision, but moving inexorably closer, were not only Simon, not only Sonia Dark, but all six members of Solo Team – present, correct and about to be put out of their misery. Bond Team's fingers tightened on their triggers.

'What are they doing?' Ben murmured, largely to himself. 'They're all bunched up together. They're making themselves easy targets.' Was it some sort of trick? He wouldn't put deceit of any sort past Simon Macey, but Ben found it impossible to guess what advantage Solo Team could gain from keeping so close to each other.

Ben shook his head in bafflement. 'Christmas must be early this year.'

'Yeah,' added Jake, 'and here come the turkeys.'

Yelling at the tops of their voices, Solo Team charged. Their rifles crackled, stasis bolts lancing through the innocent forest air.

'They haven't seen us. They can't have seen us. What's going on?' Cally turned to Eddie.

'Maybe they don't like the look of that bush,' Eddie suggested, 'the one they're blowing to bits.'

'Wait for it,' hissed Ben. 'Let them come on a little further.' Then he'd have Macey in his sights.

Solo Team stopped. They seemed stunned, stupefied. Simon Macey looked at something in his hand, shook it vigorously. Solo Team clustered around him.

This was as good as it was going to get.

'Fire!' cried Ben.

A barrage of stasis bolts ripped through Solo Team. They didn't even have time to raise their own rifles. Huxley was paralysed instantly, stiffening and toppling, out of the game. So was Johns. Conrad caught fire from front and rear, jerked, spun, fell.

Bond Team were on their feet now, scenting total victory.

But they weren't encircling the enemy, not entirely. Simon saw his chance. He grabbed Sonia Dark. She swore and she struggled but neither were helpful. She took the stasis bolt intended for Simon. Then he was letting her go, hurtling away as she fell, his stasis rifle forgotten, a reckless fugitive.

Out of range.

'Blast!' spat Ben. 'Let's get after him.'

'No!' Jake's urgency made everyone pause. The blaze in his eyes brooked no contradiction. 'Macey's mine.'

Simon's panic was making him stumble, slowing him down, and he wasn't thinking straight, either. What had gone wrong with the tracer? Everything had been looking so perfect and now he was blundering about in the forest in a team of one. And he could hear a pursuer. It'd be Stanton, stasis rifle at the ready to claim his victory. And without his own weapon – Why had he dropped it? Stupid – there was nothing he could do to prevent it.

But he could sure take the gloss off. Maybe it was time Stanton learned the truth about his pretty little girlfriend.

Simon slowed to a halt, raised his hands in surrender, turned to face Ben Stanton with a sneer. Which quickly became a frown. It wasn't Stanton, after all. Instead, that retard Domer, Daly. Who didn't seem to be slowing. 'All right, I give up.' Jake kept coming. 'I said I give up, are you deaf?'

Jake powered into Simon Macey and the two of them thudded to the ground.

'What do you think you're doing, you moron?' Simon writhed but Jake was on top of him, fists bunched. 'I give up! Just shoot me and have done.'

'Not yet, scumbag. We need to talk.' It seemed Jake also needed to land one or two punches on Simon Macey's reddening face. 'Actually, I need to talk and you need to listen.'

'What? You're . . . insane!' Simon blurted. 'This is against the rules!'

'Yeah?' Jake thrust his face closer to Macey's. His eyes burned with such rage they might have scorched the other boy. 'Well so is planting a tracer on a member of another team.'

Macey blanched. His lips quivered. 'I did no such thing. You can't —'

'No lies, Macey – just listen!' Jake clamped his hands around Simon's throat. 'I know about you and Lori. I know you've been using her and exploiting her. And in my book, buddy, that's lower than dirt, and where I come from, that's worth the kind of pounding I'd really like to give you now.'

'Get . . . off . . . me!'

'But I'm going to be reasonable with you, Macey, just

this once. You can keep your good looks. You can keep your teeth in nice even rows. But if you *ever* open your mouth to anyone, I don't mean just Ben, I mean *anyone*, about what you did to Lori, *ever*, then one dark night when you least expect it you and me are going to meet again, and then I'm not going to be reasonable, and you won't be charming anyone else for a very long time. Do you understand me?'

A kind of gurgle from Simon Macey. Throttling tends to impair the communication.

'I can't hear you.' Jake reluctantly let go of Macey's throat. 'Do you understand?'

'. . . yes . . . *Yes!* I . . . understand . . .' Simon coughed fitfully.

'Good. Then it looks like we're about done here.'

Just in time, too. 'Jake, what's going on?' The others had arrived.

'Oh, nothing. Nothing important.' Jake got to his feet, hauled Simon Macey to his. 'Simon had a little bit of a fall, that's all. And he's got something he wants to say to you, haven't you, Simon?'

Lori's eyes widened in sudden alarm.

'What is it, Macey?'

Simon shared his defeated glare between Jake and Ben. Pointedly, he didn't even glance at Lori. 'Yeah, I've got something to say. I give up. It's all over. Stanton, the Sherlock Shield's yours.'

EPILOGUE

The ceremony was exactly as Ben had imagined.

The whole school was assembled in the Hall of Heroes, teachers and students alike. Grant was there, of course, Corporal Keene in the uniform he obviously kept clean for non-combat occasions, Lacey Bannon, Mr Korita, even old Gadge, who clearly had no idea why but at least refrained from talking to the wall during the speeches. A special screen had been installed for Jonathan Deveraux's contribution. The student teams from both year groups sat on one side of the Hall, with those Spy High graduates not otherwise occupied on missions ranked behind them.

Only Bond Team sat apart from their peers. Because only Bond Team were there to be awarded the Sherlock Shield.

Ben didn't listen much to the speeches from Deveraux and from Grant. All the talk of honour and achievement, of setting standards and living up to examples, it wasn't that he disagreed with it or even that he'd heard it all before. Ben simply wanted to luxuriate in the moment, to revel in it, to imprint the scene so indelibly on his mind that it would seem as if it might last forever.

The admiring gaze of the graduates whose ranks he'd soon be joining, the envious eyes of Hannay Team, Palmer Team and Solo Team – especially Solo Team, with Simon Macey in particular looking like he'd swallowed a lemon with more to come. This was right. This was good. This was why he'd joined Spy High.

When Grant called for 'the leader of this year's winning team, Ben Stanton of Bond Team, to step forward and collect the Sherlock Shield', Ben could have done it with his eyes closed. He'd rehearsed this moment countless times in the privacy of his own head. The reality didn't disappoint.

'Thank you, sir,' Ben said. He shook Grant's hand (or did Grant shake his?). He took hold of the Sherlock Shield. He held it high. The applause he accepted as his just deserts. When they made the film of his life . . .

The others joined him, a little unnecessarily, he thought. There were smiles all round, hugging, back-slapping, general congratulations.

And correction: smiles nearly all round.

Jennifer could have been on the same diet as Simon Macey. She wasn't enjoying the audience's adulation at all. Her eyes were darting to the exits as if she was considering making a break for one of them any second. Unstable, Ben reflected, definitely unstable, but at least she hadn't dragged the team down.

Whatever Jennifer's problem was, it couldn't hurt them now.

Later that evening, the girls were preparing themselves for the Sherlock Shield Dance. Bond Team, needless to say, were guests of honour, and Cally and Lori were planning their outfits and appearance with all the precision of a field operation. Jennifer, on the other hand, was not. Jennifer seemed to be doing nothing but sitting cross-legged on her bed and staring grimly into space.

'You not feeling well, Jen?' Cally asked. 'The pressure of the occasion too much for you?'

'I'm fine.' Each word like a shutter slammed.

'Then aren't you getting changed?' Lori wondered. 'The party'll start without us.'

'I'm not coming to the party,' Jennifer said, with a scorn that stopped both her team-mates in their tracks.

'You're not? Why?'

'Oh, I wouldn't want to cramp your style, Lori. Wouldn't want to get in your way.'

'What?' Lori didn't understand. Where was Jennifer's sudden vitriol coming from? 'What do you mean?'

'Nothing.'

Lori looked for Cally's support, who shrugged, mystified. 'Wait a minute, Jen, you can't make pointed comments like that and then just say "nothing". Have we got a problem I'm not aware of? Have I offended you somehow?'

'You know,' Jennifer snapped petulantly.

'I don't know,' Lori claimed. 'Enlighten me. Cal, do you have any idea — ?'

'Jake. It's Jake. You and Jake.'

'What do you mean, me and Jake? It's me and Ben, Jen, haven't you noticed by now? Blond guy, tall, leader of Bond Team, actually. Jake's just — '

'Someone you exchange meaningful glances with,' Jennifer accused. 'Someone you secretly meet in the grounds.'

'Oh.' Either she and Jake had been slack, or Lori could quite understand why Jennifer deserved her place at Spy High.

'Yes. Oh,' said Jennifer.

'Lori?' Cally regarded her team-mate quizzically.

'Listen, Jen, you've got it all wrong.' Lori launched into the truth but not the whole truth explanation. 'What you saw . . . I had a bit of a problem. Jake was the only one who could help me out. And he did. He helped me sort myself out. As a friend. That's it. There's nothing else, no romance, if that's what's worrying you. Ben's my boyfriend. You can see that, can't you?' Jennifer looked as if she couldn't see that. 'Listen,' Lori tried a different approach, 'it's you Jake likes, Jen. He told me so himself.'

'You see?' Cally joined forces with Lori. 'What did I tell you before? You mean you didn't talk to him?'

Jennifer's hostility began to waver. 'I was going to, but then I saw . . . and then I thought . . . So I was really horrible to him.' She regarded her team-mates with dismay. 'Jake's going to hate me now, isn't he?'

'Oh, I don't know,' Lori pondered. 'I reckon if you do something like get round to the boys' room right now and hint that you're available to be escorted to the party, Jake might be persuaded to volunteer. Like drooling, tongue hanging out kind of persuaded.'

'You think so?' Jennifer laughed. She was a different person.

'We think so,' Cally confirmed.

'Then I guess I'd better go, then.' Before she lost her courage again. 'See you in a bit. And Lori, Cally.' Jennifer smiled. 'Thanks.'

Cally watched her leave. 'The path of true love never runs smoothly,' she observed. 'Now Lo, what was this problem that only Jake could help you with?'

Jennifer ran along the corridors. She had the crazy idea that if she didn't get to Jake absolutely as soon as possible something would happen and she'd never see him again. Certain events in her life that haunted her dreams had made her pessimistic, bleak, but here was a chance for something good, something positive. And now that the business with Lori was cleared up, no one could stand in her way.

Except maybe Senior Tutor Elmore Grant, whom she nearly knocked off his artificial feet. 'Hey, where's the fire?' He wasn't taking it personally.

'Sorry, sir. I need to . . . see someone.'

'Me, too, as it happens. You, Jennifer.' He handed her an envelope, addressed to Jennifer Chen at the Deveraux College. 'This came for you today. I meant to give it to you earlier, but what with the ceremony and everything . . . we don't get much actual post these days, do we? All e-mails and videphones. Modern life, I supp— are you all right, Jennifer?'

'Yes. Of course.' She wasn't. 'Thank you. For this.' It was from Aunt Li. She recognised the writing. It couldn't be good news.

'Well, I expect I'll see you at the party, then, Jennifer.'

She didn't reply. She didn't see Grant leave. The world around her darkened, dimmed, and she could only see the letter. Jennifer fumbled the envelope open. Aunt Li did not waste ink.

He's back.

Of course he was. Of course. Jennifer felt that she couldn't breathe, couldn't stand, couldn't think. She groped at the wall for support. *He's back.* She knew he would be someday. It just happened to be today.

She felt the gorge rising in her throat, but there was nothing to be done. Tears stung her eyes. No time for Jake now. Time only for one thing.

'So are we a happy boy then?' Lori finally managed to break away from Ben and have a word with Jake between records. She was mildly surprised that he wasn't up and dancing like everyone else. She was more than mildly surprised that he was alone.

'What do you mean? The Shield? I guess if Ben shares the credit around . . .'

'No, dummy. Jennifer. You know? Tall, dark and gorgeous? Where is she?'

'I hoped you were gonna tell me,' Jake admitted. 'Isn't she with you?'

Lori frowned. A sneaking sense of foreboding crawled like an insect up her spine. 'She was supposed to be coming to see you in your room, to ask you to the party.'

'She didn't.' Jake matched Lori's concern. 'I haven't seen her since the ceremony. When was this?'

'Ages ago. I mean, Cal and me thought you'd both gone off or something. She never came back. She's not around here somewhere, is she?' Lori sought for Jennifer in vain.

'No, she isn't,' Jake said. 'I've looked.'

The music started playing again, loudly. Ben was waiting for Lori to rejoin him on the dance floor. Cally and Eddie seemed to be practising wrestling holds. Suddenly, Lori didn't feel much like partying. Something was wrong.

'Maybe she changed her mind. Maybe she's just gone back to your room.'

'Maybe.' Lori nodded thoughtfully. 'I think I'll go and check. You want to come?'

'Try stopping me.'

'Hey, Ben,' called Eddie, as he watched a bemused Ben stare after Lori and Jake rushing from the room. 'I'd look out if I were you. Could be you're losing your touch!'

'Jennifer? Jen? Are you in here?'

The fact that Lori had to turn on the light suggested not.

'So where is she, then?'

'Wait, Jake. Look. A note.' Lori retrieved the single leaf of folded paper from the middle of Jennifer's bed. She read it. She paled.

'Well?' prompted Jake. 'What does it say?'

'She's gone, Jake.'

'What do you mean? Gone where?'

Lori's expression was grave, final. 'Jennifer's gone.'

THE FUTURE
IS FANGED ...

The moon was dying.

It hung low in the night sky, as if it hardly had the strength to keep itself from falling, and it was the sickly paleness of an invalid. Its luminescence did not so much shimmer as flicker, an aging light bulb needing replacement. Which was not so very far from the case, of course. The moon that rose above Undertown Los Angeles was entirely artificial.

The brainchild of a former city mayor, the man-made orb had originally been conceived as a crime-prevention measure. Undertown was already sinking into the gutters of lawlessness and fear. Good people were moving out; gangs were moving in. The hovering moon was intended to be a beacon of hope, a shining reminder that the rich and powerful citizens of the city Uptown had not yet forgotten their less fortunate brethren Undertown. The moon's light was supposed to drive away the darkness and keep the streets safe to walk. Cameras were going to be fitted beneath the satellite's skin to cast a benevolent eye on all.

Only the money had run out. The mayor lost office. Not even a single instamatic had ever been installed. The moon's maintenance budget had been sliced to the bone, to the marrow of the bone.

The moon was dying, but it didn't seem to matter much. Undertown was in a far worse state.

At least, that was the way it seemed to the girl. The streets that she'd known so well, the sidewalks that had tumbled and teemed with life once upon a time, when she'd been small and smiling, were now dark and cold and empty. All right, it was late, past midnight, but the girl could sense dereliction in the air, and decay, and despair, like food left to rot.

And in this tomb of silence, she sensed footsteps behind her, footsteps following her. Three pairs, trying to be stealthy but heavy on the sidewalk. Males. Pursuers.

The girl narrowed her brilliant, emerald eyes. She doubted they wanted to ask her directions.

As if afraid to view what might happen next, the moon dimmed, yellowed like jaundice.

The girl heard the footsteps increase their pace. She didn't look round. She'd see their faces soon enough.

Briefly, the moon rallied, blooming a sudden, perfect white. Then there was a rattle, an electronic sigh. The power failed and the moon was blown out like a candle. It was truly night.

The girl stopped. Her pursuers didn't.

'Hey, girlie!'

The girl put down her bag. She felt she might need both hands free for this.

'Are you talking to me?' She saw them now as they caught up with her, swaggered around her, admired her lithe figure and sweep of hair as dark as the night. A United Nations of muggers, one black, one white, beneath the eruptions of acne, and one Chinese like herself. He was the biggest.

"What are you doing out here all alone . . . ?"

". . . Yeah it's late and you look like you should be tucked up in your bed."

"Don't you know these streets is dangerous?"

"Is that so? Thanks for telling me. I'll bear it in mind."

"So how's about showing some gratitude, then." They

shuffled into position, in front, behind, to the right, cutting off any escape route. To her left was the wall.

"Your bag, girlie. We want your bag." The tone was threatening now. Their muscles tensing.

"And anything else that's going."

"Everything else!"

"Well," said the girl, "you'd better come and get it, then."

She took the Chinese guy down before he could even flinch – a lightning karate chop. The black guy behind, she'd expertly judged his height, and directed her kick accordingly. The white guy, eyes wide, went for a knife. The girl went for him. Twisted, yanked. Even a knife wouldn't help with a dislocated arm.

With her would-be assailants groaning on the ground, the girl assumed a defensive posture. Though she also assumed she wouldn't need it. She was right.

"Who are you, girlie?" The muggers groped to their feet, kept their distance. "You shouldn't be here, the likes of you." They staggered back down the street, broke into a shambling run. "You don't belong here. You don't belong!" Their final call, and more painful to the girl than anything they could have done physically.

Because she *did* belong here. Right here.

As the moon clicked into life again, like a happy ending, the girl gazed up at the apartment building alongside her and her cat-green eyes filled with tears. She did belong here.

Jennifer Chen had come home.

SPY HIGH Episode Three:
The Serpent Scenario

Available from July 2003
www.thedeverauxcollege.com
www.spyhigh.co.uk
www.atombooks.co.uk

THIS TIME IT'S PERSONAL!

SPY HIGH
Series One

EPISODE ONE:

The Frankenstein Factory

Release Date: May 2003   ISBN 1904233139   £5.00

EPISODE TWO:

The Chaos Connection

Release Date: May 2003   ISBN 1904233147   £5.00

EPISODE THREE:

The Serpent Scenario

Release Date: July 2003   ISBN 1904233155   £5.00

EPISODE FOUR:

The Paranoia Plot

Release Date: September 2003   ISBN 1904233163   £5.00

EPISODE FIVE:

The Soul Stealer

Release Date: November 2003   ISBN 1904233171   £5.00

EPISODE SIX:

The Annihilation Agenda

Release Date: January 2004   ISBN 190423318X   £5.00

www.spyhigh.co.uk
www.thedeverauxcollege.co.uk

www.atombooks.co.uk